APOKALYPSIS

By James R. Snyder

Apokalypsis

Foreward

Writing is a craft, like any other. It takes time, patience, and above all – practice.

Practice, practice, practice.

I like to think of myself as a creative person. I enjoy all the creative outlets – art, music, film, books, etc. I love coming up with an idea, picturing it in my head, and then executing it in whatever medium suits my creative juices. It could be composing a piece of music, drawing a picture, planting a flower bed, decorating the house for the holidays, or even writing a story.

Sometimes, the idea comes out exactly as I have envisioned it in my mind.

Sometimes there are happy accidents.

I've always considered myself a "closet" writer. It's one of those skills that I know I possess, but probably don't nurture it in the way that I should.

Then came National Novel Writing Month, or NaNoWriMo, as it is affectionately known.

I discovered NaNoWriMo back in the early 2000's. Its premise is simple. 50,000 words in 30 days.

The story can be anything. It can ramble – it can be total nonsense. The whole purpose of it is as a creative exercise. The folks at NaNo encourage you to "turn off" your self-editor (actually, there's a whole other month just to edit – earlier in the year). Write as if no one else will ever read what you're putting down on paper. If its garbage? Throw it away. No one will know, no one will look down on your work, - treat it as practice.

Treat it as working on your craft.

The 50,000 words thing? That, too – is just arbitrary. It's just a number to shoot for. It's a goal and a target for folks (like me) who have a difficult time writing without some sort of deadline.

This is my third attempt at NanoWriMo. My first two attempts never reached the 50,000 word mark (this attempt barely made it), but for a brief moment – I had a story and wrote it down - from start to finish. That in itself is an accomplishment. These works may never be the "Great American Novel" or ever see the light of day (other than for close friends and family), but to me – it's fulfilling. Like the painter who adds his last brushstroke to a finished piece, the musician who plays the last note, or the dancer who takes their bow following a performance, it is a closure. It's not a "what if" or "I should have" moment – it's an "I did this" moment.

My experience with NaNoWriMo has also helped me craft other pieces of writing. I've dabbled in some poetry (though it's also probably all crap), written some short stories, and even authored a blog for a time – all because of the encouragement I received from and chance I took with National Novel Writing Month.

Oh, and that craft thing? How one has to practice to get better? It is so true.

I'll admit it – my first NaNoWriMo story? Garbage (at least I think so). The second one? Solid (but short). This attempt? Too fresh off the presses for me to reflect upon yet, but no matter if I love it or hate it in the years to come, I have learned to embrace the process. Let the creative juices flow. Let the mood or story take me where it will. It is VERY freeing.

I've written some good short stories since my first NaNoWriMo days. I'm my harshest critic, but I read some of these now and am proud of the work. It stands up.

I look at it and feel good – it's an intangible happiness – a combination of confidence, accomplishment and satisfaction.

Everyone should have that feeling - at least once in their lives.

I encourage you, dear reader, to take that leap.

Always wanted to play the guitar?

Do it.

Always thought it would be fun to make a quilt?

Do it.

No matter what inspires you or interests you – take the time to explore it. Not for anyone else – not to be published, seen, or heard.

It should be just for you.

So sing in the shower, doodle on your napkin, or try to bake bread.

If it inspires you – explore it.

Thank you, NaNoWriMo. You've shown me a way to release my pent-up creativity, and I'm a better person for it.

Jim Snyder

November 2014

For Leigh, Becky, Catie, and Mom

CHAPTER 1

Tony Perez was not in a good mood. He was just coming off of a ten day vacation from his job at Quest Services, Inc., a private computer outsourcing firm that provides operational and infrastructure support and services for a wide variety of global companies. Vacations were never long enough, Tony thought, as he buzzed in past the security desk and took an elevator up to the 3rd floor Operations Center. As soon as one started to relax, it was time to come back to the daily grind.

 Tony had a high stress position at Quest Services, Inc. He was an incident manager, which meant that he was on the front line for any critical problems or issues that came up on a daily basis. Companies relied on their IT infrastructure and services to work 24 x 7 x 365 days a year, and when they stopped, Tony and his team would get a "severity one" call, which meant that one of the supported clients was experiencing a high profile outage or problem that was impacting their business.

Quest Services supported all types of companies, from small retail operations to large, global conglomerates. Every company had its own quirks and critical needs, but what they all had in common was that when there was a "SEV1" issue, people panicked – and complained – loudly. Outage time could mean customers wouldn't have access to a company's website or be able to buy something from their online store. In the modern business model, that meant that those companies were losing money during an outage – and that meant that sooner or later, some executive was going to contact Tony and give him an earful.

Tony stopped at his cubicle and turned on is laptop. Over seven hundred emails had accumulated in his account while he was on vacation. He then punched up the Quest monitoring tool and took a quick look at all of the current activity. There was a lot going on. Several outages were already being worked on – some of them for a while now. Catching up on email would have to wait. He grabbed a quick cup of coffee from the break room and headed out to the Operations floor. It was a large, dimly lit rectangular room with no windows and high ceilings. The lower light allowed the monitors which filled the outside

2

walls of the room to show up better. Banks and banks of video monitors showed various systems, network paths, and operational messages scrolling across dozens of screens. Operators manned small stations in front of these large banks of monitors around the room, responding to messages, warnings, and executing various system commands. Surprisingly, all of these monitors and systems could be supported by only a few trained people.

In the center of the room were two half-moon shaped consoles that faced each other. Each had multiple workstations embedded into it, and they were manned by several people wearing headsets who were busy talking on the phone and staring intently into their screens. One side acted as a customer service desk, where end users would call-in to report problems. The other side was for incident management – Tony's area.

Tony slid into his seat and signed into the system, putting on his headset and plugging into the desk phone. His arrival was a welcome one, because the 3rd shift incident manager, Cheryl Hinds, was busy talking on the phone, looking drained and glad to see that the day shift relief person was on the scene.

That meant only one thing – there was a bad outage going on. Tony was going to be thrown right back into the fire - so much for easing back into work after his vacation. He glanced up at the monitoring screen and saw a red entry for 'AnyWayAnyDay', a Russian airline company that Quest had been supporting for about two years. Tony glanced at the duration of the problem thus far – six hours and counting, and knew that it was going to be a bad morning. Oh well, nothing to do now but face the music. He got Cheryl's attention.

"Ready for turnover whenever you are," he said in an unenthusiastic voice.

"Welcome back," said Cheryl. "I've got a doozy for you this morning – I hope you plan on being glued to your chair all day," she added.

"Give me the rundown," Tony said, sighing.

"DNS problem – a bad one," said Cheryl. "IP addresses aren't resolving."

"Localized or bigger than that?" asked Tony.

"It's big," added Cheryl.

DNS stood for "Domain Name Service". DNS was the way that computers talked to each other over a network connection. The DNS was a unique set of numbers which identified a specific computer to the network. All computers have a specific DNS. Think of it as a phone number. In order to reach a specific person on the phone, one has to know their specific phone number. The same goes for DNS. In order to talk to a specific computer, one has to know its unique DNS – and be able to reach it. This allows the IP addresses of the specific hardware to create a connection and "speak" to each other.

"What's the impact?" asked Tony.

"Also bad," explained Cheryl. "Their online booking engine has been down for over six hours now. They haven't been able to book any flights, and their terminal agents are also unable to access the central reservations systems at various airports. They are basically dead in the water. There are planes sitting on the ground and it's causing flight cancellations up and down their system."

"Uggh," said Tony, "- are they saying how much revenue is being lost?"

"You know these companies," said Cheryl. "At six hours? They are throwing around numbers in the millions now."

This was going to be a long day. "Who's on your call?" asked Tony, grimacing,

"Well, I have good news and bad news," said Cheryl. "The good news is I've got the Intel Level 3 support person, the DNS Subject Matter Expert, two guys from Network Ops, three supervisors and an Account Exec from our side on the conference call. They've been pounding away at the logs and network routes for hours now."

"And the bad news?" asked Tony.

"Someone gave out the conference call number to the client, so you've got the higher-ups from the customer side on the call, throwing a fit," she added. "They've been very helpful," she added – very sarcastically.

"Perfect," said Tony. "Let me get dialed in."

Tony dialed into the conference call, introduced himself, and announced to the participants that he would be taking over from Cheryl as the incident manager running the problem. He then asked for a summary on where they currently stood regarding the issue.

"Still nowhere," said the Intel technician. "We can't log into any of the servers because of the DNS problem, but our onsite support personnel report that the servers themselves appear to be running fine – we just can't sign-on remotely to anything."

"Where do we stand with the DNS support team?" asked Tony.

"I've never encountered anything like it," said the DNS expert. "I've got a case open with both AT&T and Microsoft, but so far they've got nothing. Our network folks also state that the network itself appears to be OK – all the switches and routers are up - we just cannot get anywhere on it – DNS just won't resolve to anything."

"It's the same story we've heard for hours now. I don't think you all have any idea what this means to our business," a heavily accented Russian voice interrupted. "We are losing thousands and thousands of dollars for every minute that these systems are down, and you don't seem to have a clue as to what's causing it."

It was obviously the client chiming in. This was going to make the resolution even harder, because now the end-users could hear everything that was going on – both good and bad. Technical calls always ground to a standstill whenever the client got on. Customers always wanted to offer solutions or direction that had nothing to do with the problem at hand. Executives were used to barking orders and getting people to respond, but on calls like these, they were nothing but problematic.

"I appreciate your position," said Tony, tactfully, "-understand that we are doing everything we can at this point."

Tony also had also joined in on a conference meeting on Quest Services' instant messaging system. This allowed all of the Quest technicians involved on the call to communicate to each other via text messages. The Intel support person, DNS Subject Matter Expert, Network support, and other Quest employees were already there. Tony quickly typed a few lines of text into the ongoing conference meeting.

"Clients on the call — be careful what you are saying — they can hear all. Oh, and don't take anything personally — they are just blowing off steam."

He did not want anyone to accidentally say something on the conference call that would shine a poor support light on Quest Services, or give the client any fuel to attack Quest's customer service while this issue got fixed. He knew the client's patience was at an end, and that the technicians were on eggshells because of the customer's presence on the phone. When angry executives joined a call and starting spouting off, the technicians generally went into "silent mode", so instead of giving any information at all, they simply clammed up completely, which often made it even worse for clients, who were starving for **ANY** kind of update or information.

"We've tried rebooting the DNS servers, I assume?" asked Tony.

"Twice...," said the Intel support tech, "- with no success. The system comes back clean, but DNS is still down."

"What's our ETA on hearing back from Microsoft and AT&T?" asked Tony.

"Supposed to hear back from them within the hour," said the DNS expert. "I can try to get them on the call, if you think that would help."

"I want them here!" shouted the Russian client representative.

"Sir, I'm going to have to ask you to calm down. Let's get Microsoft AND AT&T on this bridge as soon as we can – I think it will help in the diagnosis," said Tony. "Meanwhile, do we know if there were any recent changes to the system?"

"I checked the change records," said the Intel technician. "These systems haven't had any work done on them for the past three weeks."

"Any known virus or bug reports out on our supplier websites for any of these DNS or server versions?" asked Tony.

"All clear there as well," said another technician. "If anyone else has experienced an issue like this, they haven't reported it."

Tony was trying to think of anything else he should have checked at this point. It appeared as if he had all of the bases covered. All they could do now was to wait until someone from Microsoft or AT&T joined in on the call.

"What is happening?!?" shouted the Russian. "Where is Microsoft? Where is AT&T? We are losing money by the minute while we sit here and wait!"

"Sir, again, I understand your concerns but we have to wait until the right people are engaged here to move forward at this point, said Tony, remaining calm. "It should only take a few minutes – "

"We don't have a few minutes!" interrupted the Russian. "I want the next level of support engaged on this line immediately! I am the CIO for this company and I want some answers! Your inability to resolve this problem is impacting our business!"

Tony's patience was nearing its end. His pet peeve was when a customer tried to throw their title around, like it meant that the techs would suddenly have a different answer. The Russian CIO had unfortunately crossed the line.

"Sir," said Tony, this time a little more forcefully, "- again, we understand that this has impact to your business, but no matter if you are the CIO or the janitor at your company, the answers we have provided you are still the same. Now, you can either be part of the solution or you can be part of the problem – and right now you are being part of the problem. Am I making myself clear?"

"Who do you think you are talking to?" roared the CIO. "I'll have you pulled off of this account!"

The CIO was following the "standard" playbook in these situations. Demand action - throw around the company title - then threaten the underling's job. Tony had heard this scenario so many times and he was in no mood for it today.

"Sir, if you can't control yourself, I will take my teams off of this line and onto a private bridge," said Tony, with quiet force and determination. He could be a prick when he needed to be. "Then you'll have no updates whatsoever. Now – I am telling you for the last time - calm down and be quiet. Unless you have some sort of technical input to the discussion, I'll ask you to not speak anymore."

There was a slight pause at the end of the line.

"I'll discuss this with your supervisor after this is all over," said the Russian, who was quietly seething, but the ultimatum worked. He went silent.

"That's fine," said Tony. At least he got the Russian to shut up. His instant messaging conference lit up with comments from the technicians, ranging from smiling emoticons to several short messages of thanks.

Tony knew he was going to hear about it later, but at least he had the call back under control.

A few minutes went by and the Russian chimed back in.

"What did you do? My teams are reporting that the systems are coming back online!"

"Team?" asked Tony. "Can I get a confirmation? Did you do anything on your end?"

"We haven't done anything," said the DNS person. "It looks like DNS is resolving again on its own. The IP addressing is fine and stable. Server communication is coming back up. We're working on confirmation now."

"I can also confirm access," said the Intel technician. "I can remotely sign-in to the servers. There doesn't seem to be anything unusual in the error logs. It looks like it came back on its own. One minute we couldn't reach or see anything on the network – now we can."

"Can we get client confirmation?" asked Tony. He was directing his comments towards the CIO.

"Our online portal is responding as designed," the CIO chimed in. "Our field agents also report that the reservation systems are coming back online. We're also working to get our stuck planes back off of the ground."

"That's good to hear," said Tony.

"We still don't know what happened," said the CIO.

"At this point, none of us do," said Tony, in sincere honesty. "That will have to come out in the post-mortem. For now, I think we are all glad that the system is back up and running as designed."

"Da," said the Russian, forgetting to speak in English for a moment. "Thank you for your help."

"You are welcome," said Tony. "I'm going to close out the call now – our people will be in touch."

He eagerly hung up the phone.

This one was a puzzler. They hadn't done anything, yet all of the DNS resolutions were suddenly working again. He looked at the time and noted it in the ticket logs. 6 hours and 23 minutes of outage. The problem had mysteriously disappeared as quickly as it had appeared. What could have caused it? There would be hell to pay on the root cause analysis if this was Quest's fault, but for now, Tony could close out this call and ticket and get back to catching up on his email.

Thousands of miles away in another data center, another supervisor was also reporting that the DNS problem with 'AnyWayAnyDay' was also resolved.

He entered a glass-enclosed office that looked out over a humming computer room, bustling with activity.

"Epsilon test completed and successful," said the supervisor. "All systems are reporting nominal and online."

A large, high-backed chair swiveled around from a bank of monitors. Its occupant was pleased.

"Any problems in the delivery?" said the high backed chair.

"None," said the floor supervisor. "Everything executed according to plan – no issues upon insertion."

"Excellent," said a voice from the shadows. "Notify our field teams. Proceed with the next phase of the operation – as scheduled."

"Yes, sir," came the quick reply.

The chair turned back to the monitors, and in the glow of the screens, its occupant grinned.

"And so it begins……."

CHAPTER 2

It was a beautiful morning in Cornwall, England. The
seaside village of Port Isaac was a picturesque town on
Cornwall's northern shores. Postcard beautiful, with
craggy outcrops and old cobblestone houses which
hugged the tops of the cliff walls, Port Isaac had become
famous as the fictional town of 'Port Wenn' in the BBC
series 'Doc Martin'. Its narrow streets were busy in the
summer with visitors and tourists who wanted a taste of
the world inhabited by their favorite fictional general
practitioner.

In the fall and winter, though, it was just another small,
Cornish village with nothing but the locals, who
appreciated the break form all the gawkers and guests.
Most of the small B&Bs were unoccupied at this time of
year, and many of the quaint shops were shuttered during
the cold weather months.

 Simon Duphrane loved the off-season. He had lived in
Port Isaac for more than ten years – not long enough to
be considered a local, but long enough not to be stared at
in the pub as a stranger. In Simon's opinion, the town was
at its most beautiful with fewer people in it. Modern
technology had allowed him to perform his duties as an IT
consultant from anywhere on the globe, and to him, Port
Issac was just about as good as it could get. Simon only
had to pop into London to the main office about once a

month for meetings with his direct supervisor and a few clients. It allowed him to keep touch with the civilized world, but offered him the freedom of performing his day-to-day duties in a corner office of his cottage that overlooked the bay.

On this fall morning, Simon has finished his morning routine of catching up on email and phoning a few clients. The sun was shining and from his window, small whitecaps could be seen on the water. A perfect day for a cliff stroll, thought Simon – and why not? Working from home had its perks, and this was one of them. No one to watch his every movement - as it would have been if he worked in a cubicle farm in some drab London office.

Simon grabbed his windbreaker and set off from the cottage. The breeze felt wonderful on his face. Simon could hear the waves crashing in the bay and taste the salt spray in the air, even from this distance. He made his way up a rocky path that flattened out into a small rise which continued towards the cliff face. There was a bench at the cliff's edge up ahead that was one of his favorite spots to sit and take in the entire scope of Port Isaac and the bay, and he could hear the seabirds screaming from the rocky outcroppings below as he continued on the path and across a green, moss covered field towards the cliff's edge.

Simon noticed a person was already sitting on the bench. Apparently, someone else had the same idea as he did – wanting to take advantage of the glorious view. Simon approached the bench and addressed its occupant.

"Good morning," said Simon, "- do you mind if I join you?"

"Not at all," said the stranger. Simon had never seen him in the village before.

"Just visiting, I take it?" said Simon.

The stranger smiled. "Yes, just passing through," he said. "What a beautiful spot."

"Oh yes," added Simon. "It's my favorite spot to sit in all of Port Isaac."

"I know," said the stranger.

Simon was puzzled by the response.

"I'm sorry, do I know you?" said Simon.

"No," said the stranger.

The stranger calmly reached behind his back and pulled out a small hand gun – equipped with a silencer. He fired two shots into Simon, who slumped forward on the bench - still with a look of complete surprise and disbelief on his face.

The stranger patiently allowed Simon to fall forward onto the ground, replaced his weapon, and checked Simon for a pulse to make sure he was dead.

The stranger then began frisking him. He quickly found Simon's wallet, which he rifled through, looking for a particular object.

He soon found it.

The stranger removed a small, non-descript plastic keycard from Simon's wallet. It had no markings on it except for a single line of large print letters on it in black which read "NUMBER 6". He then placed the key-card inside a small metal box which he pulled from his own pocket. Finished with his search, the stranger replaced Simon's wallet in his pocket, removing nothing but the key-card.

He then quickly dragged Simon's body to the edge of the cliff and rolled it over the side. The stranger gave a small salute to the corpse as it took flight and in a few seconds, it landed among the rocks with a bone-crunching thud, one hundred fifty feet below. The stranger then walked away as the cliff birds screamed and the surf howled.

CHAPTER 3

The headquarters of the FBI's Cyber-Crime Division was tucked away in a basement corner of the FBI's central office at 935 Pennsylvania Avenue in Washington, D.C. Although there were several "official" field offices assigned to the cyber-crime unit, most of these "field offices" were merely a spare desk in an otherwise unrelated government agency office in most of the major cities across the U.S. If the Washington, D.C. headquarters was supposedly the model office in the fleet, it certainly didn't show it. A non-descript cluster of gray cubicles with a surrounding bank of walled offices, it looked like any other office environment in today's business environment.

The work and investigations being done here; however, were far from ordinary. All sorts of cyber-crime - from internet scams to hacking to child pornography - eventually filed though this office. Lower level cases were filtered out to the various field offices, but cases with more of a national impact (or political fall-out) stayed in the Washington, D.C. bureau and were worked by the field agents in this office.

Alan Silverman was one of those agents.

A husky red-head of medium height, forty-year-old Alan has been with the Cyber -Crime Division for the past ten years – four of which were in this pit of an office that had earned the appropriate nickname "the cage". People who worked in "the cage" were treated a little differently. No one else in the building tended to socialize with the cyber-crime unit due to their long, odd hours and the secretive nature of their work. Wild stories would often come out of "the cage" about various supposed cases the team was involved with, but no one internal to the team would ever confirm or deny them to an outsider. Everyone who worked there seemed to all thrive on the mystery – and the distance – that the department afforded them. The unit also tended to favor loners and agents without families. Divorce rates were high, and Alan had added to that total. His wife left him soon after he transferred to the Washington D.C. bureau four years ago, which came as a surprise to no one. Alan probably hadn't been home for more than two nights in a row for the past eight years, and he loved to work the weekends when even fewer people were around to bother him.

Alan was known to have a keen intellect and sarcastic manner, and while prized by the bureau for his case results – his personality made him hard to work with. Alan tended to shoot from the hip with his opinions and comments, and that often left co-workers, teammates, and department heads with a bad taste in their mouths. At his age, Alan really didn't care about impressing people anymore, and it was clear that he would never go too high up the government management chain due to his caustic nature.

Alan was busy in his cubicle working on some research and leads on the recent credit card number hacks for large retailers such as Home Depot and Target. Those crimes had gotten huge publicity in the press and on network news, but Alan knew it was just the tip of the iceberg regarding stolen credit card information. He used to tell people all the time that no credit card was safe.

"If you have a valid credit card, I can almost guarantee you it's been compromised by someone somewhere – they just haven't used it yet," he would tell anyone willing to listen – but no one ever did. People just couldn't fathom the possibility - or believe it, even if it was most likely true.

Reggie Winters, another agent in the unit, poked his head into Alan's cubicle.

"Hey Alan, I hear a new case is coming in," said an excited Reggie. Reggie was always excited about a new case. Then again, most twenty-five-year olds were excited about nearly anything.

"Can't you see that I'm clearly busy?" said Alan, not even looking up from his notes.

"Some Russian airline thing," continued Reggie. "I hear its hot stuff – aren't you interested?"

"Why are you still speaking?" said Alan, head still down in his work.

Reggie drifted off to bother another co-worker with the gossip. A few minutes later, the phone on his desk rang. He ignored it. Soon, there was a knock on his cubicle entry. It was his boss, Janet Chalmers.

"I tried to call you," said Janet, obviously perturbed. "Didn't you hear it?"

"I did," said Alan, still bent over his desk and scribbling notes.

"I need to speak to you in my office," said Janet.

Alan still continued on with his work.

"Now – as in today," said Janet, her voice rising a little in frustration.

Alan calmly stopped working, whirled around in his chair, and got up. He stopped at his cubicle entrance and in front of Janet, extending his hand and bowing.

"After you, madam," he said with a bow.

Janet turned on her heels and rolled her eyes, leading Alan back to her office.

She took a seat behind her desk and motioned for Alan to take a seat.

"I've got a new case for you," she began.

"I've got plenty of cases piling up on my desk right now, thank you," said Alan.

"I'm not asking you," stated Janet, quite firmly, "- I'm telling you. This one comes from high up. A Russian airline company just had a total DNS failure – and no one knows why."

"Reggie was babbling about this thing earlier," said Alan. "What do we care about a Russian company with a DNS issue?"

"I don't know," said Janet, "- but someone cares – and they want my best agent on it – and unfortunately for me - that's you."

"You charmer, you," quipped Alan.

Janet slid across a folder with the details.

"This is top priority and is to take precedence over all of your other work," she added.

"Until the next top priority comes along," Alan added, picking up the folder. He got up to leave.

"Keep me posted," said Janet.

"I'll send you a nice note every afternoon, dear heart," dead-panned Alan as he left the room.

"Another bug hunt," thought Alan as he headed back towards his desk. He posed his previous question again to himself. "Why does the US government care if a Russian airline company went "tits up" on their DNS?" He sat back down in his chair and pushed his other work aside, opening the folder and beginning to read the overview. Reggie popped his head back in.

"You got the Russian thing, didn't you? I saw you in Janet's office."

"Actually," said Alan, "- we talked about you. Janet asked if we had anyone we could let go and your name came up."

Reggie was surprised, scared and then angry – all in the space of five seconds.

"You know what, Alan?" said Reggie. "You're an asshole." Reggie's head disappeared.

Alan chuckled to himself and nodded.

The sun was setting over Victoria Harbor in Hong Kong. The Central Business District was slowly winding down from another business day. Inside a data center on the North Shore of Hong Kong Island; however, technicians were busy gearing up monitoring systems and preparing for another exercise.

"All systems green for the Theta test execution – on your order," said the floor supervisor over the intercom system.

The large swivel chair that overlooked the data center floor turned to face the monitors and staff of the Operations Center. Its occupant was drinking hot green tea from a delicate china cup. He took one long, last look at all of the monitors and gave a satisfied sigh.

"Execute," the voice commanded.

CHAPTER 4

The headquarters of Amazon, Inc. is atypical of what many would consider a "normal" corporate office. Nestled in the heart of Seattle, Washington, it is only a short walk away from such tourist destinations as the Pike Place Market (where fish mongers actually throw large salmon and other fish for gawkers to catch), the Seattle Aquarium, and the world-famous Space Needle. The office complex itself blends right into its urban neighborhood setting.

The campus is divided into two distinct buildings, "Day 1 North" and "Day 1 South". Each building has various floors of workspaces, each resembling more of an upscale dormitory than a 'Fortune 500' office environment. Thick, comfy lounge chairs dot the work areas, small kitchenettes break up the official office spaces, and the hallways are lined with eclectic art.

This laid-back atmosphere belies the sheer scope and size of the company. Over eighty-nine worldwide warehouses service over two hundred million customers. More than one billion items were shipped in 2013, over thirty-seven million on the Monday after Thanksgiving alone (known in the U.S. as "Cyber-Monday"). The company did over seventy-four billion dollars of net sales in 2013, making it a marketing and retail giant.

The data center for Amazon is also state of the art. More science fiction in tone than a typical facility, the 2nd floor Operations Command Center resembles the bridge of a starship or futuristic naval vessel. State of the art flat screen and touch sensitive panels surround individual monitoring ports, where a single operator can monitor and control up to seven screens simultaneously. Each operator communicates via a tiny blue-tooth enabled headpiece, so they can get up and move around the room at will, not shackled to their desk area by a restricting cord. The floor is dotted with multiple monitoring cells which all feed to a central control station. The lead operator here can call up any screen from any monitoring cell - and can also throw that monitor's display up onto giant one hundred twenty inch flat-screens that make up the far wall of the command center. From this central command, Amazon can monitor all of its warehouse operations, track its internet traffic and sales, and obtain real-time data on package delivery to anywhere in the world. Several of the large flat-screens on the far wall are reserved and produce a giant world map. On this map, all of Amazon's worldwide warehouses and hubs are visible - the network connections between them are illustrated by lines showing the basic connections between the hubs.

This morning was a good one so far. All of the hubs and connecting lines were green in color, indicating that all of the connections were online and functioning as designed.

Ignacio "Nacho" Ramirez was the floor supervisor of the command center on duty this morning. Nacho liked green. Green was good. Green meant no problems. He took a sip of his latte and scanned over the various monitoring cells. It was a well-oiled machine – all of its parts and components working as designed.

It started slowly and innocently enough.

The dot indicating the location of Amazon's fulfillment center #TPA1, located in Ruskin, Florida changed from green to red. The operator working the southeastern U.S. monitoring station took note of the change and began to investigate. First, she checked the Amazon change system to see if there were any scheduled outages for that location. No tickets were listed. She jotted down the system time that the dot went from green to red – 08:17 PST – on a pad of paper she kept on her monitoring console. She wasn't worried. Sometimes hiccups in the monitoring system would cause a location to turn from green to red because the monitoring script missed a cycle of had some other sort of anomaly. If the dot changed back from red to green in a minute or two, she'd know it was just a false alarm.

After two minutes, the dot was still red. Growing concerned, she tapped a few keys on her console and spoke into her blue-tooth set.

"Hey Mike, this is Lisa over in Southeast - - you reporting any network issues or power outages in Ruskin?"

"Hey Lisa – good morning," replied Mike. "Let me check."

Lisa patiently waited and watched her screen. Ruskin was still glowing red.

"Lisa, I'm not getting any reports of power outages, but I can confirm that we can't reach Ruskin," said Mike. "I'll let you know if I discover anything."

"Thanks, Mike," said Lisa. "I'm going to get a trouble ticket opened."

Lisa switched one of her view screens over to the Amazon problem management system - called 'Maximo' - and began to type in a trouble ticket. This ticket would be routed to the proper support group (most likely Mike's over in the Network area) and investigated. She finished sending out the trouble ticket and went back to her main view screen.

Fifteen minutes later, the dot indicating Amazon fulfillment center #LAL1 in Lakeland, Florida changed from green to red. The network connection line from Lakeland to Ruskin also switched colors from green to red. Lisa made a few keystrokes on her console.

Nacho Ramirez's headset began to buzz at his central command post. Hey keyed on his headset.

"Central Command, this is Nacho, how can I help you?"

"Nach? This is Lisa over in Southeast. You'd better bring my area up on the big board. We may have a problem," said Lisa.

Nacho typed in a few keystrokes of his own. Soon Lisa's map of the southeastern U.S. displayed up on one of the one hundred twenty inch view screens. It clearly showed the red indicator lights for Ruskin and Lakeland, as well as the red network connection between them.

"You have a ticket open?" asked Nacho.

"Yup-" said Lisa, "– Mike over in Network Ops is looking at Ruskin now – Lakeland just happened."

"OK," said Nacho.

Nacho keyed in Mike's headset number.

"Mike? Nacho from Central – what's the story down in Florida?" asked Nacho.

"Don't know yet," replied Mike. "We can't reach anything there – we're still checking. Give me a few minutes."

"Keep me posted," said Nacho.

As hey thumbed off his headset, another call came in.

"Nacho? It's Barry in Midwest. We've just lost three fulfillment centers – two in Plainfield and one in Indianapolis."

While he was listening to Barry, Nacho could see that another call was coming in. He glanced up at the big worldwide map on the far wall.

To his amazement, locations all over the U.S. were starting to turn from green to red. The spider-like network lines that indicated each area's network connections were also starting to turn from green to red. Nacho got a knot in his stomach. This was not good. He keyed up Mike again in Network Operations.

"Mike what's happening? I'm starting to see connection losses and fulfillment centers go offline all over the U.S.?" Nacho's voice was beginning to rise.

"We're getting killed over here, Nach," said Mike. "There's something up with DNS. We can't get any server or location to resolve. It's like they are all completely dropping off of the network map." Mike was also beginning to show concern in his voice.

Nacho glanced back up at the worldwide map. Locations were changing from green to red all over Western Europe, Asia, and South America. The network lines were starting to look like blood-filled veins fanning out over a large body. Nacho was beginning to flop-sweat. This was very,

very bad. He keyed the headset to speak to the entire Operations Center over the intercom.

"Team, this is Nacho in Central Command," he stated, trying to calm his voice. "As you can see from the big board, we have a major situation here. We're losing sites and connectivity all over the grid. Techs, I need some answers – the sooner the better, please."

All around the monitoring room, heads were raising up to look at the big board. Overall, it was showing more red now than green - and getting worse by the minute. To add to the problems, the monitors that indicated the company's website traffic were also beginning to turn from green to red. Internet traffic to and from Amazon's web servers was being choked off.

There was no explanation. The wave of outages was growing by the second. Every headset on the monitoring floor was buzzing. Every monitoring cell had flashing alarms. People were shouting. Some stared with disbelief at the big board. It was like nothing they had ever seen.

At 9:03 PST, someone looking at the big board shouted loud enough for almost everyone to hear.

"That's it! – it's all down!"

The large world map told the story. Every Amazon fulfillment location was showing red.

Every - -single - -one.

The network connections between all of the centers were also red. All of the network paths for Amazon in the entire world were down.

All internet traffic? Down.

The red reflected across the room, casting a crimson shadow over the Operations Command Center.

Nacho looked like death warmed over. The bile churning in his stomach was in his throat. The sweat pouring off of his brow was clearly visible. He had spent the last ten minutes having his rear-end handed to him by the CIO of the company. They wanted answers - they wanted the problem fixed – and they wanted it yesterday.

The network technicians were frantic and all on the phone, trying to uncover what was going on, but DNS was dead. No one could contact any of Amazon's servers or locations. It was as if the entire library of net addresses had been completely wiped from the system.

Every minute of outage time was costing the company hundreds of thousands of dollars.

Amazon was dead in the water. Not a single penny of commerce was flowing through it.

CHAPTER 5

At a Hong Kong data center half a world away, the monitoring screens were also showing red, but unlike the operators in Seattle, here everyone seemed to treat it as an expected result.

This time, Wu Li Chang, the Operations supervisor, personally walked up the stairs to the observation area to report the good news. The large swivel chair was turned away from the Operations Command Floor, its occupant instead scanning the several monitors mounted on the office walls.

On one was a feed from CNN. The network was reporting on a major worldwide outage to Amazon's website and online ordering systems. The screen "crawl" at the bottom of CNN's feed indicated that Amazon officials were confident that they had the problem well in hand and would have it resolved soon.

The seat's occupant chuckled as he read the remark, taking a long drag on his hand-rolled cigarette, the smoke creating a pleasing curl above the high back of the black leather chair.

Wu Li cleared his throat, announcing his presence to the room's other occupant.

"Yes?" came a voice from the chair.

"Our test was 100% successful, sir," reported Wu Li. "Amazon has been completely neutralized. They cannot access any of their systems and their internet traffic is now down to zero."

"Excellent work, Wu Li," said the voice. "Give my compliments to your team."

"How long do you wish the test to continue?" asked Wu Li.

The chair was silent for a moment. Only another curl of smoke rose up from behind its high back.

"Let's keep our friends crippled for another thirty minutes," said the voice, "- then they can be restored. Proceed with the next phase as well."

"As you wish," said Wu Li. He turned and left the observation area.

The chair and its occupant returned to scanning the various monitors on the walls. On the Al-Jazeera feed, there was a report of renewed fighting between the Ukrainian army and Chechen rebels. The chair's occupant raised a crystal glass and took a long pull of vodka from it. He grimaced and clenched his teeth as he swallowed, watching the images.

"No one cares," he said out loud - to no one in particular.

"But soon, the entire world will wish they had." He took another pull on his cigarette - its smoky curl slowly rose above the chair in a lazy arc.

CHAPTER 6

Nacho Ramirez was a beaten man. The CIO of Amazon had basically asked for his resignation if he could not resolve the problem that was currently crushing Amazon's ability to make money.

He was standing in the Network Operations area, which is where the only work was going on in the Operations Command Center. Everyone else could only stand and watch as the five network technicians worked the phones and scanned log after log on the system, trying to determine what happened to all of their DNS connectivity. With no DNS resolution, there was no way that any computer on the network could talk to one another. It would be the same as a person in Boston trying to talk to another person in Los Angeles by shouting into thin air. There was no way the message would get through.

The Network team had tried to create new DNS server entries, but the system would accept the command and then do nothing. AT&T had their 3rd level support person involved, and Microsoft had a team of experts on a call, but every idea that had been tried thus far was resulting in failure.

Nacho excused himself and went out into the hall to go to the bathroom. He entered the men's room, splashed some cold water on his face at the sink, and then vomited his entire breakfast into the first empty stall. He was on his knees in the bathroom, flushing the toilet when he heard the door to the bathroom slam open.

"Nacho, get in here quick! Everything is coming back online!"

Nacho flushed the toilet, got to his feet, and splashed a second round of water on his face. He looked at himself in the mirror. He was ashen and pale, but the news he had just heard was the best thing that had happened to him all day and it seemed to calm his stomach a bit. He tucked in his shirt and slowly made his way back out onto the Operations floor.

It was like a different room. The monitoring cell technicians were all busy at their stations, responding to alarms and once again, shouting into their headsets. Over in the Network Operations section, two technicians were actually hugging.   Nacho glanced up at the big board.

One by one, location indicators and their associated network connectors were turning green.

Nacho glanced over at the internet monitoring systems. They too were turning green, and the number of active connections was starting to climb. That meant that people all over the world were signing in.

 Signing back in to Amazon – and shopping again.

Nacho waited thirty minutes until the worldwide map was his favorite color again. Then he made the call to the CIO.

"We're back online," was Nacho's simple statement.

"Great job," was the two word reply from the CIO, who then hung up the phone.

Great job? Nacho hadn't done a thing. As a matter of fact, none of his people had done a thing. The system had come back on its own – and to Nacho, that was the scariest part of the story.

Amazon had been crushed – and no one knew why.

CHAPTER 7

The thirty foot fishing boat 'Try Your Luck' slowly made its way out of Maracas Bay on the north side of Trinidad. Nevil Rockledge, a thirty-five-year old programmer, originally from London, had been living in the islands for the past five years. Nevil's successful participation in a recent online start-up had allowed him the freedom to work whenever and wherever he felt like it.

Today, Nevil did not feel like working. Today, Nevil wanted to fish.

Specifically, Nevil wanted to fish for tarpon, and there was no better place to fish for tarpon than in the waters of the Bocas, off of Trinidad's northwest coast. Nevil had hired the boat for charter just yesterday. He was going to have some friends along, but decided he would enjoy the day on his own.

There would be no one on board except for Nevil, the boat's captain, John-Pierre, and John-Pierre's first mate, Phillipe.

Nevil stood in the stern of the 'Try Your Luck' and watched as the docks and port of Maracas Bay slowly disappeared in the morning sunlight. It was a perfect day on the water, and he took a seat in the deck chair and was becoming increasingly relaxed by the slow and steady sway of the ship.

"Mr. Nevil, can I get you somtin' to drink, man?" said Phillipe.

"A Red Stripe would be perfect, Phillipe, thank you," replied Nevil.

Phillipe disappeared below decks and returned with the short squatty bottle of a Red Stripe beer. It was ice cold. Nevil took a long pull from the bottle and exhaled a satisfied sigh.

"How long will it take to reach the fishing grounds?" asked Nevil.

"Cap'n say tirty to forty-five minutes," smiled Phillipe.

Nevil gave him a "thumbs up" and took another long pull on his beer. This was the way to live. Nevil was finding it hard to understand why he hadn't discovered this peaceful island life earlier in his career. Lucky for him, his seventy-to-eighty hour work weeks were behind him. The future would be full of fishing trips, long naps, and lazy evenings on his veranda back on shore.

The gentle rocking of the ship combined with the warm breeze caused Nevil to comfortably sink deeper and deeper into his chair. His eyes were becoming heavier and heavier and he was soon fast asleep.

Nevil was awakened into consciousness by a sharp pain around his neck. As he opened his eyes and tried to get his bearings, the pain around his neck intensified and he could not breathe. He reached his hands up to feel a taut cord stretched around his neck, pulling ever and ever tighter. His eyes were wild and he desperately tried to reach behind him. As his hands fumbled across a face and shoulders and as he struggled, he caught a quick glimpse of his assailant.

It was Phillipe, pulling hard on the cord and smiling.

Nevil continued to struggle, but he couldn't wiggle his way out of the chair or Phillipe's crushing grip. His Adam's apple felt like it would be launched down his throat. He tried to shout, but nothing came out. His movements became wilder and less coordinated. His vision was blurring and becoming dark around the edges.

Nevil Rockledge was dying, and he knew it.

The spasms of his limbs were becoming less and less violent, and Nevil started to black out. All along, Phillipe continued to apply pressure. The cord was now cutting into Nevil's skin, and a small trickle of blood began running down the front of Nevil's chest.

Nevil stopped struggling, growing limp in the chair. Phillipe continued to hold on for another minute, making sure the job was complete. When he finally released his grip, Nevil's neck had a strong black-and-blue ring from where the killing pressure had been applied.

"Is he dead?" came a voice from the pilot house.

"Yeah, mahn," said Phillipe. "He's done for."

"Good," said John-Pierre. "Get what we need and get him over the side."

Phillipe went over to the side of the boat. On a bench there, Nevil had brought a small gym bag with his personal things – a change of clothes for later in the day, some sunscreen, his ID, and one item of interest to Phillipe.

A non-descript plastic card key.

On its side in large block letters were the words "NUMBER 3".

Phillipe pocketed the card, picked up the bag with Nevil's personal belongings, and tossed it over the side.

Nevil soon followed.

The 'Try Your Luck' continued on out into the Bocas. Jean-Pierre and Phillipe would soon spend the rest of their morning drinking Red Stripe beer and fishing for tarpon.

After all, the charter was paid for – why waste it?

CHAPTER 8

Alan Silverman had a headache. He'd been pouring over the provided system logs from 'AnyWayAnyDay', the Russian airline company that had recently experienced a crippling DNS outage (at least the ones the Russians had reluctantly provided) and he couldn't figure out why the Domain Name Service wasn't resolving.

Domain Name Service (or DNS) originated in the mid 1980's. It was an easier way to recognize the increasing number of servers and other hardware being added to the then growing internet. Any piece of hardware - whether it is a printer, router, laptop, or large corporate mainframe – is considered a host. Each host can have a unique name, such as "Printer1", "Lynksis28954" or "AndersonLaptop".

Each host then resides in a specific domain. Domains can contain several levels. At the top level, the domain name has a suffix which we are all familiar with today in the internet world. Examples of this are ".com", which is used for commercial organizations, ".org", which is used for non-commercial organizations (think PBS, etc.), and ".gov", for government related sites.

DNS essentially acts as a distributed database, allowing the domain name (such as "mywebsite.com") to map to a specific IP address, which is the unique numeric identifier of the host to the network. So, in the example above, "mywebsite.com may have an IP address of "123.456.789.000". Numeric IP addresses are easier for the numeric world of the internet, while domain names are easier for humans to remember. Without DNS and its associated IP resolution, the internet is essentially blind and cannot find anything.

From the logs Alan was looking at, there was no indication or clue as to why DNS wasn't working for the Russian airline company. One minute it was working as designed – the next minute it wasn't. It had also resolved itself the same way. One minute it wasn't working – the next minute it was. It was a complete mystery to Alan thus far, and Alan didn't like mysteries.

The phone on Alan's desk rang. He could see it was a call from Janet Chalmers, his boss. Normally, he didn't answer the phone, but he was stuck at the moment and needed a break. He picked up the receiver.

"Domino's Pizza, this is Alan – can I take you order?" he said briskly into the receiver.

"Very funny," said Janet, surprised that he had even answered. "Can I see you in my office, please?"

"OK," replied Alan. "I'm coming over." He hung up the phone and stepped away from his desk. It felt good to get up and stretch his legs, anyway.

He knocked on the doorway and poked his head in. Janet was seated at her desk. Across from her in one of the two guest chairs sat a young, green-eyed brunette who was speaking with Janet. She had on a smart business suit and carried a small folder. They stopped their conversation in mid-sentence and stared at Alan in the doorway.

"Ahhh, Alan – there you are – please come in and sit down," said Janet.

Alan came in and took the seat next to the new girl.

"Alan Silverman," said Janet, pointing her hand at Alan. "I'd like you to meet Wendy Tosca – she's with the NSA." She then motioned over towards the girl.

Wendy reached out her hand, and Alan did as well, completing the handshake. Wendy had a firm grip and looked him straight in the eye.

"Nice to meet you, Alan," said Wendy. "I've heard a lot about you this morning."

"Lies, all lies – every single one," said Alan, jokingly. He glanced over at Janet who was not amused.

"Wendy is one of the NSA's computer experts, specializing in cyber-intelligence," said Janet.

"A woman in cyber-intelligence?" said Alan, raising his eyebrow towards Wendy.

"Wow – that's very observent ," said Wendy, sarcastically. "What gave me away – the skirt?" Alan was sure he saw Janet suppressing a grin out of the corner of his eye.

"No offense," said Alan.

"None taken," chimed in Wendy. Her expression hadn't changed and she didn't appear to be upset by Alan's comment.

"Wendy has some additional information about your Russian airliner case that you need to hear," said Janet.

"I'm listening," said Alan.

"You may or may not know yet, but Amazon had a huge system outage this morning," said Wendy. "They were crushed for about an hour or so – I mean completely off-line. They've done a pretty good job of down-playing it in the press – so far."

Alan hadn't heard about it yet. Of course, he'd been staring at system logs all morning. Still, if Amazon had a major outage and the media hadn't pounced on it as of yet, there was a PR person somewhere in Seattle that deserved a raise.

"What kind of outage?" asked Alan.

"That's the part you're going to find interesting," said Wendy. "It was a total DNS failure."

The hairs on the back of Alan's neck stood up. In the IT world, outages with the same symptoms were not a coincidence.

"What?" said Alan, looking over at Janet for confirmation. Janet shook her head in agreement.

"I've got a similar story with this Russian airliner outage I'm looking at," said Alan.

"I know," said Wendy, "- but what you don't know is that there are more than just these two cases," she continued.

Now Alan was genuinely interested. He was leaning forward in his chair with keen attention to Wendy's new details.

"Along with the Russian airliner outage, over the past few weeks we've had reports of several other DNS-related outages for several other companies. Each one has shown the same symptoms," explained Wendy. "The systems are running fine, then for no known reason, DNS just stops resolving, killing their ability to communicate with any other server or piece of hardware. After a prescribed time, the problem just disappears."

"So the NSA obviously thinks this is deliberate," said Alan.

"Deliberate and coordinated, Captain Obvious," added Wendy. "The size and scope of each company attacked has increased with each incident."

"Which would lead one to believe that something worse is in our future," said Alan.

"I'll hand it to you, Janet – the boy is quick," said Wendy.

Alan was a bit startled by Wendy's tone. It had been a long while since he got as good as he gave in the sarcasm department. It was refreshing – and it relaxed him a bit.

Janet turned to address Alan directly. "This is why I've called you in, Alan," said Janet. "The NSA is looking for an FBI partner to assist in the investigation, and since you've got the Russian airliner case – "

" - and since I'm your best agent - " interrupted Alan.

Janet stopped for a moment and gave him a glare. " - and since you were assigned the Russian airliner case, you'll be partnering up with Wendy here to get to the bottom of this thing."

"A partner?" said Alan, looking over at Wendy.

"Easy, lover boy – we won't be picking out china together at IKEA. It's just a work case," said Wendy.

This time Janet did not suppress her smile.

"Well, I see you two are going to get along just fine," said Janet. She got up and extended her hand to Wendy, signaling that the meeting was over.

"Wendy, if you need anything, please let us know," said Janet. She purposely ignored Alan. "Good luck."

Wendy turned to leave. Alan stood there for a second and Janet sat back down, returning to the work on her desk. Alan continued to stand there, frozen for a second.

"Is there a problem?" said Janet, looking back up at Alan.

"Me? Uhh, no – no problem," stammered Alan.

"Then I'm sure you and Wendy have work to do," added Janet, looking back down at her desk papers. She was grinning again. This was turning out to be a memorable day for her.

Alan dropped his shoulders a bit and recognized that the conversation was over. He turned to follow Wendy out of Janet's office.

Alan returned to his desk and found Wendy sitting in his seat, reviewing his system logs from the Russian airliner case.

"Uhh, pardon you - but the visitor's seat is over there," he motioned to another small chair in his cubicle, away from his desk.

"Sorry," said Wendy. "I just wanted to take a look at what you had. It's nice to see what other agencies pick up on these kinds of cases." She moved over to the visitor's seat and waited for Alan to take his.

Alan re-adjusted a few papers on his desk that Wendy had moved.

"A little ADHD are we?" asked Wendy, still staring at Alan.

"Not at all, I just have a system and you're messing with the system," said Alan a little irritated. He continued to shuffle papers around. A few seconds went by. Wendy finally broke the silence.

"Don't you want to ask me anything about Amazon?" she inquired.

"Tell me about your background," said Alan, still annoyed. "I need to know how technical I can be with you," he said smugly.

"Oh, goodie – a job interview," said Wendy, not the least bit concerned. "Let's see, I graduated from the Naval Academy in 2001 with a degree in Computer Science. I did my Navy stint in cryptography and cyber-ops – got out in 2006 and was recruited into the NSA. I've done two years of field work all over God's creation and am now back in the labs and in the field, working on cyber-threats and other computer monsters that go bump in the night. How's that, Sherlock?"

"Easy, girlie," added Alan, bowing down in mock reverence. "I offer thee a truce, fair maiden."

"I shall accept, gallant knight," responded Wendy.

They both smiled.

"I take it there were no symptoms or clues in the Amazon attack – DNS just stopped?" said Alan.

"Right," said Wendy. "I was just checking your logs on the Russian incident to see if you'd seen anything different. Obviously, we are both still grasping for answers."

"When in doubt, go see the experts," said Alan.

"Agreed," said Wendy. "Who first - - yours or mine?"

"Age before beauty," quipped Alan, indicating they would visit his "experts" first.

"Lead on, grandpa," said Wendy, "- try not to break a hip before we get there."

CHAPTER 9

The Symantec Corporation makes software administering the safety and security of computer systems around the world. In fact, it is probably far and away the leading supplier of security software to Fortune 500 companies both in the United States and throughout the globe.   It provides security solutions such as 'Norton Antivirus', 'Enterprise Vault', and the 'Veritas' suite of software which provide safe and reliable security solutions for servers, networks, databases, and peripherals.

Due to its wide variety of products, teams of technicians are constantly trying to stay one step ahead of hackers and other malicious code, creating and supplying security updates for literally millions of workstations, laptops, and network devices. These updates are routinely shipped and downloaded to subscribing clients all over the world.

Garrett Hamilton was one such programmer. Garrett had been one of the lead architects and designers on the 'Norton Antivirus' suite of software for more than three years. Norton was probably the best known and widely used product from Symantec, so keeping current and ahead of the security curve for Norton products was a prized and pressure filled position.

Teams of programmers for Norton constantly scanned the internet for reports of viruses or other malicious activity.

Their job was then to get a copy of the virus itself (sometimes by taking a system and letting it become "infected"), analyzing the code, and then creating a program or subroutine to counter-act its ill-effects.

Once a solution was devised, it was packaged up with other fixes and then sent out as a package update to the millions of subscribers of Norton software products. Most of the time, end-users were completely unaware that their software was even being changed. Norton pushed out its updates to paid subscribers over the internet. The new code would become incorporated into the existing code already residing on an owner's system, ready to respond to any documented threat it may eventually encounter.

Software updates are sent out whenever necessary, although they are generally held and distributed on a monthly basis – unless there was some emergency situation. This was to prevent overloading local networks with outgoing updates as the software was "pushed" to the end user community.

Garrett was looking at the whiteboard in his office. It contained a list of all of this month's new software updates and fixes for Norton. So far, there were twenty-seven enhancements listed on the board, addressing a wide variety of problems and issues.

A knock came on the doorframe of his office, and he looked up to see a wire mesh mail cart parked in his office doorway. A fresh-faced intern was holding a large bundle of letters, manila envelopes, and other communications.

"Mail call, Mr. Hamilton," said the young intern.

"Thanks, Stacy," said Garrett. "Just drop it on my desk there, if you please." He motioned towards the least cluttered corner of his desk.

The intern left to continue her rounds and Garrett turned away from the whiteboard to take a look at the day's mail. It was hard to believe in this day and age there was still so much paperwork. The day's mail was filled with shiny adverts from software companies pitching their latest add-ons to Norton (would Garrett be interested in meeting with one of their sales people?), industry magazines, and assorted other fluff that was destined for the "round file" – the wastepaper basket at the end of his desk.

As he quickly thumbed through the stack, one item caught his eye.

It was a blank postcard – addressed correctly to him but containing no note or return address. The only marking on it was a stamp and postage cancellation mark from Hong Kong.

The postcard had one word printed on it.

"Apokalypsis"

Garrett suddenly froze, turned the postcard over, and then turned it back, as if more would be revealed. The single word continued to stare back at him.

"Apokalypsis"

Garrett was suddenly a little weak in the knees. He sat down and stared blankly at the far wall of his office. He swallowed hard, turning his head quickly around his office, as if searching to make sure no one could see him looking at or holding the postcard, which he constantly went back to as he scanned the room. There was no one else in the office but him.

He took one last look at the postcard, then shakily reached over and dropped it into his document shredder. It flicked on and greedily consumed the card, casting its remains into the bin below.

Garrett felt a little better that the card was gone, but the signal had been sent and the message was very clear.

It was time.

CHAPTER 10

Alan and Wendy arrived in Los Angeles late in the afternoon. They had caught the first flight they could get out of Washington, D.C. and had just enough time for each of them to throw together an overnight bag which they had stowed in the overhead bins of their cross-country United Airlines flight as carry-on luggage. Their side-arms were safely tucked away into their holsters and out of view from the general public (after clearing them with the TSA authorities). They were not expecting trouble, but one never knew out in the field. Once on the ground, they grabbed a rental car and were headed towards the Playa Vista section of Los Angeles.

Their destination was the headquarters of the Internet Corporation for Assigned Names and Numbers, or ICANN for short. A non-profit organization, it was ICANN's task to organize and coordinate the Internet's global domain name system. If there would be any organization that had an idea of what was going on with the recent rash of DNS issues, it would be ICANN.

Alan pulled into the ICANN offices, an unremarkable set of low buildings in a Playa Vista office park.

"Who exactly are we here to see, Dad?" said Wendy, playfully. They were getting used to each other's ways on the flight out.

"Fellow by the name of Martin Boyle," replied Alan. "He's with the department responsible for managing the root DNS system and numbering system for IP addresses. We go back a ways."

"Old frat buddy?" said Wendy.

"Something like that," said Alan. "Take is easy on him, he may not warm up to your charms," he added in, holding the door for Wendy to enter the office complex.

They were standing in a plain, utilitarian lobby. A central desk contained a receptionist, and there were a few chairs set up as a waiting area along one wall. A set of key-card entry doors kept visitors from wandering any further into the complex - unless they were invited.

"Can I help you?" said the receptionist, an older Hispanic woman with severe glasses and graying hair.

"Yes - -," said Alan, "- I'm Agent Silverman of the FBI and this is Agent Tosca from the NSA," he continued. Both he and Wendy made a cursory flash of their badges for authenticity. "I'm here to see Mr. Boyle, if he's available. He should be expecting us."

The receptionist gave the badges a glance, then motioned them towards the chairs along the wall.

"Have a seat," she said, in thickly accented English. "I'll let Mr. Boyle know you are here." She dialed the reception phone as Alan and Wendy sat down.

They had not been seated long when they heard a buzzing of the security doors and Martin Boyle entered the room. He was tall and thin, with dirty blonde hair graying at the temples, but perfectly styled and in place. He was wearing small, expensive-looking reading glasses, a silk bow-tie, and white lab coat. He crossed the room and extended his hand to Alan, smiling.

"Alan, my friend – how are you?" He shook Alan's hand briskly, who returned the smile and enthusiastic handshake.

"Fine, Martin – just fine," he replied. "Long time – no see."

"Tell me about it," said Martin. "How long has it been since I've seen you - - four years?"

"Probably closer to five," added in Alan. He motioned over to Wendy.

"Martin, this is Agent Wendy Tosca, from the NSA's cyber-division," continued Alan. Wendy extended her hand to Martin.

"Pleasure to meet you, Mr. Boyle," said Wendy, continuing with the pleasantries.

"Please, my dear – Martin – call me Martin, I insist," he said, still smiling. "Mr. Boyle is my father, who is long gone." Wendy smiled back at him and nodded.

"Wendy is helping me on a case," said Alan, "- and we in turn could use your help, if you have a few minutes."

"Anything for you, Alan," Martin stated. "Let's step back into my office, shall we? Maria, can we get a couple of visitor IDs for the agents, please?"

Maria, the receptionist, handed over two ID badges labeled "Visitor" that were attached to long lanyards. Alan and Wendy slipped the lanyards over their heads and around their necks so that the badges were clearly visible.

"Now, right this way," Martin motioned for them to follow him. He swiped his ID card over the entry pad and the doors clicked to the unlock position. He opened the door and escorted them through.

He led them down a series of corridors and into a more plush office, one that was fit for an executive. The mahogany chairs here were far more expensive, and thick carpeting covered the floor. A large sofa was also in the room, creating a small sitting area separate from the desk area. A floor to ceiling window revealed a small garden space at the end of the office, and the gurgling of a fountain could be heard in the distance. Martin directed

Alan and Wendy to two seats that were opposite the couch.

"Swanky," said Alan. "I see you've kept your expensive taste over the years."

"Indeed," said Martin settling into the couch, "- and why not? I spend a lot of time in this building – no reason that I shouldn't do it in some sense of comfort, when it's available."

Alan gave a slight nod of approval. Wendy glanced over at Alan and raised an eyebrow. Alan shook her off with a "not now" glance.

"Can I offer you anything? Herbal tea? Spring water?" asked Martin. Both Alan and Wendy shook their heads no, so he continued. "Well then – what can I do for you?"

"You understand that what we speak about here today is considered essential to an ongoing case and therefore considered privileged information – not to be shared," stated Wendy.

"Of course, dear," said Martin, moving forward on the couch and innocently touching her on the knee. She again looked over at Alan, who gave her a reassuring look to let her know that there was nothing to be feared from Martin, at least not for her gender. Wendy got the gist of Alan's subliminal message and relaxed a bit.

"Martin, you may have heard that there have been some high-profile IT outages recently," said Alan.

"I think I remember seeing there was a Russian airline company that had issues," replied Martin, "- that one was all over the news – and Amazon had something happen recently as well. Why, have there been others?"

"Quite a few," chimed in Wendy. "What the general public doesn't know is that they all seem to have a common thread. Their DNS systems were temporarily compromised and suspended."

"Hmmm," thought Martin, out loud as he slid back comfortably into the couch. "Any indication in the system logs as to what may have happened?"

"None that we can see," added Alan. "The DNS resolution just seems to stop for a period of time, then re-starts after the outage all on its own."

"Any indication in the database tables of corruption post-mortem?" said Martin.

"None," said Alan.

Martin stood up and walked over to the garden window. He stared at the fountain for a few seconds with his hands on his hips, thinking to himself.

"What about the registries and address spaces," he stated, still looking into the garden. "Any block problems or issues that couldn't be resolved by a reboot?"

"Reboots didn't fix anything," stated Alan. "The issue persisted until it felt like stopping – at least that's what it looks like."

"Or someone wanted it to end," added Martin. "It sounds like someone deliberately masked the DB entries mapping the domain names to the IP addresses. The machines couldn't resolve because they didn't know what to resolve to," he continued.

"Exactly," said Alan. Martin walked back to the couch and sat down again.

"How many of these incidents have you recorded?" said Martin.

"Five," said Wendy, "- all of them increasing in both scope and duration. It's as if someone is testing something."

"Someone is testing something," Martin added, confidently. "You've just been lucky enough so far that whomever or whatever is doing this has only "masked" the database, not destroyed it. That means they have allowed DNS to recover – they could have just as easily eliminated the table – and that creates bigger problems."

"How so?" asked Wendy.

"If the database table that links the domain name to the IP address is destroyed, then whatever was mapped – a website, server, even a home printer – is gone. There's no way for the machines to talk to each other."

"Can't that be fixed?" asked Alan.

"Sure, you can manually re-map everything," said Martin. "Which is easy if it's your home computer and printer - but if you're talking about a lot of servers and hardware - not to mention all of the network equipment involved? A large company would take weeks or months to recover - possibly years if the breach was big enough."

"What about backups?" said Wendy. "Couldn't you just reload the table from a backup?"

"Load the table from where to where?" added Martin. "Remember, it's like the blind leading the blind during the outage. The DNS and associated IP addressing would have been destroyed. Unless you can reset the entire system, you can't restore from a backup if you don't know, – or can't communicate to – where point "A" and point "B" are physically or logically located. It would be a total shot in the dark."

They all sat for a few moments in silence, letting the scenario that Martin just described sink in for a bit.

"This is a problem," said Alan, finally stating the obvious and breaking the silence.

"Actually, I'm glad you stopped by," said Martin, seeming to change the subject. "I was wondering who I could talk to about a certain issue we're facing around here at the moment."

"Martin, we'd love to help, said Alan, "- but unfortunately this issue has some urgency – "

"I think you'll find," interrupted Martin, "- that both of our issues may have something in common."

Both Wendy and Alan looked quizzically at each other.

"I believe it's time," said Martin, "- to show you both some of things that we do here."

CHAPTER 11

Martin led Alan and Wendy down another drab corridor and to another entrance policed by a key-card entry door. In addition to the key-card entry, Martin also peered into a small scanner, which was affixed to the wall at eye level above the key-card reader.

"Identity confirmed," said a soothing, female electronic voice. "Welcome. Martin Boyle."

Wendy leaned in close to Alan. "What's going on?" she whispered.

"No idea," Alan whispered back. "We'll roll with it for now."

The click of multiple locks was heard and the door buzzed. Martin opened it and motioned Alan and Wendy inside.

The room they walked into was small compared to most meeting spaces – only about 12 feet by 12 feet in diameter. On the far wall was a single large flat-screen panel with a map of the world displayed on it - just like the map at the Amazon Corporate headquarters. On its dlsplay, lines snaked out of various worldwide cities visible on the map and connected points all over the globe. All of the lines and their connections were currently green.

Other than the flat-screen panel, the only other thing in the room was a large circular table placed directly in the center of the space. On the outer edges of the table, seven rectangular boxes were placed at regular intervals around the outside edge – all the same distance from one another – like the hour marks on a clock face. The boxes themselves were unremarkable. Each had no exterior markings other than a single line of large block print letters. The box at the "top" of the circular table (the end next to the large wall monitor was labeled "NUMBER 1". The second box, moving clockwise, was labeled "NUMBER 2". This continued around the circular table, each of the seven boxes marked with a corresponding number. On the front of each box was a small open slot that appeared as if it was meant for a card or other peripheral to be inserted into it. Next to each slot was a small indicator light. Each light on each box currently registered a bright red.

In the dead center of the round table was a round red button, which rose up from the table's surface. A single light with a metal circular shade hung down from the ceiling and cast a glow over the entire tabletop.

Alan and Wendy looked at each other, then looked at Martin, who was practically beaming as he allowed the duo to take in the room.

"What do you think?" asked Martin, eager for some feedback?

"I don't know," said Alan, "- what exactly are we looking at?"

"The monitor on the far wall shows all of the internet traffic and routes currently set-up and functioning around the globe. Each tendril and line connecting the cities on the map is a main internet trunk line for data communications," explained Martin.

"Well, at least they are all green – I assume that's good," said Wendy.

"Indeed it is," added Martin, "- as long as everything is green, that means that worldwide communications are working and that all DNS activity is resolving correctly around the globe.

"Let me get this straight," said Wendy. "This agency controls ALL of the DNS connectivity – for the entire world?"

"Something like that," said Martin, chuckling a bit. "We control, monitor, and maintain the master databases for all of the domain name servers as they map to their corresponding worldwide IP addresses."

Wendy looked a little shocked. "All from this little room?" she added in disbelief.

"No, no," said Martin, chuckling again. "We monitor and maintain the master lists from other control rooms in this facility. We are entrusted by corporations, governments, academia – basically everyone who uses a computer around the world – to efficiently maintain and administer the worldwide DNS system."

"So what is this room for?" asked Alan.

"This is our fail-safe system," said Martin, growing serious again. "If we would ever suffer a catastrophic data corruption, terrorist attack or other event that would create a worldwide loss of DNS connectivity, we could essentially "reboot" the system from this room."

Alan raised his eyebrows in disbelief. He looked at Wendy, who was also at a loss.

"Unbelievable," said Wendy.

"How does it work?" asked Alan.

"Actually, it's quite simple," stated Martin. "The DNSSEC Root Key, which is responsible for resetting the system - should the need ever arise - has been encrypted and divided into seven different code strands. Each specific code strand has been transferred onto a magnetically protected, environmental-proof key-card. To reboot the system, five of the seven key-cards must be inserted into their proper slot here on the table."

He pointed at one of the rectangular boxes on the central table.

"Once the proper key-card has been inserted into its proper box, its code section is uploaded and this indicator light turns from red to green," continued Martin. "Once five or more cards have been correctly inserted, the red button in the middle will light up. This button can then be pressed, which will initiate a reboot of the entire DNSSEC root key and basically "restart" the internet."

Both Alan and Wendy were in a bit of a shock. This was quite a lot to take in – and they could both see why Martin was under the impression that their current cases and this facility could be very much related.

"If I may ask," said Wendy, "- just where are the key-cards?"

Alan looked over to Martin as well, awaiting his answer.

"For security purposes," said Martin, "- we distributed the cards to seven random people around the globe, which we call our "trusted community representatives", or TCRs. These are able-bodied and trusted IT professionals from around the world who understand what we do here and were willing to volunteer to take on the responsibility for this important task."

"So you just gave them the cards and said 'don't lose this'?" said Alan, a little perplexed at how nonchalant Martin seemed to be taking all of this.

"Don't be silly," said Martin. "There are protocols in place. Each TCR can be flown here within sixteen hours - if the need would ever arise - to enable the fail-safe option. We also require each TCR to check-in with our office on a weekly basis to report their location. They also share any upcoming travel plans so we can alter their emergency travel arrangements, if that is necessary."

"Sixteen hours?" added Wendy. "You'd be willing to endure a sixteen hour outage of the worldwide DNS system? Why not just keep all of the keys here? Why all the cloak-and-dagger antics?"

"The odds of destroying all of the code strands as separate entities seemed far, far less than keeping the complete strand intact," said Martin. "Our global partners also insisted that the risk be shared with other countries besides the United States. It truly is a worldwide responsibility and a great example of cooperation in our global cyber-community."

"Now you sound like an ad agency," said Alan.

"Perhaps," said Martin, who suddenly turned serious. "Now for the reason I'm telling you all of this, and its relation to the problem you have brought to me."

"We're listening," said Wendy. She glanced over at Alan. They both knew that bad news was coming.

"Remember I told you that we have protocols that require our TCRs to check in every week?" said Martin.

"Yes," said Alan.

"That's the problem," said Martin, who lowered his voice to almost a whisper, as if he didn't want the room to hear him.

"Two of our seven key holders haven't checked in. We've lost contact with them."

CHAPTER 12

"So let me see if I have this straight, Martin," said Alan, who was now past the shock of Martin's revelation and was now clearly annoyed. "You've built this elaborate Hollywood-type fail-safe system, distributed all of the components around the world to seven different people – whom you say you can trust – and now the only people who can restart the system are disappearing?"

"It's a problem, but I'm not that concerned as of yet," said Martin, trying to sound reassuring. "Our TCR contact in Trinidad and Tobago is notorious for missing his communication check-ins. He loves to fish and is often out to sea on a boat and away from any cell coverage."

"And your other missing person?" said Wendy, who shared Alan's annoyance and concern.

"That's the one I'm worried about," said Martin. "He's our Great Britain contact, and he never misses a call."

Wendy was already dialing her cellphone.

"Name and location – now!" Wendy barked at Martin – while waiting for the other end of her call to pick up. It wasn't a request, it was an order.

Martin was shocked at her sudden change in tone. He just stood there.

"Now!" shouted Wendy.

"S-Simon Duphrane," stammered Martin, still taken aback. "Port Issac – it's in Cornwall."

Wendy walked to the other end of the room and spoke into the phone.

"Martin?" said Alan, trying to coax Martin back into the present. "Martin – you have to understand. This obviously isn't a coincidence. The targeted attacks on DNS at increasingly larger companies – the disappearance of your card key holders – it's too coincidental."

"When you put it that way, its worse than I realized," said Martin, almost ashamed. "I'm glad you came in, Alan. I should have contacted you. I should have called the police. I should have – "

"Nonsense," interrupted Alan, trying to soothe Martin's bruised ego a bit. "There's no way you would have known. Now, does anyone else know about this yet?"

"No," said Martin. "I'm the one who takes the calls from our TCRs. I hadn't told anyone else yet."

"And we don't want you to," said Alan. "One, we don't want to start a panic – and two, we don't want to let on that we know what we know. Can you get us a list of the names and addresses for the other card holders?"

"Yes," said Martin. "It's published on our website."

Alan couldn't believe it. "The names and addresses of the seven TCRs are listed on your website?"

"Just the names and country of residence," said Martin, trying to defend the statement – and realizing he had blundered again. "We're a non-profit, you know – people want to see what we're doing – it's how we raise money to fund our operations here." He understood now what a serious mistake ICANN had made, even as he tried to explain it.

"Tell me the site doesn't explain your little system here," said Alan, bowing his head and rubbing one hand through his hair in anguish. "Please tell me it's not on there."

Martin hesitated, and Alan had his answer.

"I'm sorry," said Martin. "I had no idea. It was good PR……" His voice trailed off as he dropped his head as well.

Alan had seen this type of mistake before. Companies and their CEOs and CIOs were so "gung-ho" to tout a new technology or innovation that they tended to blab about it in a press release before they really knew what they were doing He recalled a situation years ago when the Walt Disney Company sent out a release praising their wireless payment technology for their Florida resort. That's all several hackers needed to fly down there and check it out. They actually sat in their rental cars in the theme park parking lots with their laptops, collecting unencrypted credit card information out of thin air.

Wendy hung up her phone and returned to the conversation. She noticed both men's heads were hanging low.

"Somebody die?" she asked.

"Almost," said Alan, raising his head. Martin kept his bowed. "What have you got?"

"We've got field agents checking on both missing persons," said Wendy. "Can we get a list of the remaining key holders?"

"Unfortunately - - that's NOT going to be a problem," said Alan. Martin's shoulders drooped a little further down.

"Martin? We need you," said Alan, placing a reassuring hand on his friend's shoulder.

Martin raised his head and walked towards the door of the fail-safe room. Wendy and Alan followed.

"I'll get you the names," said Martin, as they headed back towards his office. "The first one should be easy."

"And why is that?" asked Wendy.

"Because she lives right here in Los Angeles," said Martin.

CHAPTER 13

Dana Kaminski was enjoying a relaxing afternoon doing what she loved, shaping lifeless clay into useable objects of art. Dana has spent twenty-five long years "chasing the success demon" as she called it. He career and tenure as head of Stanford's prestigious Information Technology department had been impressive. Other Silicon Valley area colleges had gotten the jump on Stanford in the early 1980's, but through sheer will, drive, and determination – first as a computer science professor and then later as its department head – she had vaulted the Stanford IT department onto the national stage.

She had single handedly increased alumni donations to the department by a factor of seven and overseen the largest expansion of academic buildings and equipment upgrades to the campus in half a century. Stanford's shiny, new Computer Science wing was a testament and lasting legacy to her vision. Top level Stanford graduates were now sought out by all of the best IT firms, and an undergraduate degree from Stanford in Computer Science practically guaranteed employment. She had earned a well-deserved rest.

Instead, she had turned her retirement interests to other creative outlets. She had discovered pottery, and now was completely consumed by it, constantly creating new bowls, mugs, and other objects. Dana was not the kind of person who went into any hobby half-hearted, and her house had turned into a free-form studio space. She had a professional grade potter's wheel set up on the back patio of her Burbank bungalow. Racks and shelves lined the living room and dining room – filled with finished pieces, partly glazed and painted pieces waiting for firing, and boxes of unused clay and supplies. She even had a huge kiln set up in the back yard, which she used to fire and harden her own creations. The hallway walls were also lined with ribbons of all colors, testament that Dana's new career in the arts was to eventually become as successful as her previous career in academics.

Dana was at her wheel, turning out yet another clay pot. She was diligently working on slowly raising the sides of the cylindrical piece of spinning clay. She carefully applied additional water to the mound and through practiced pressure and hand movements, a round tower magically rose from the wheel. Dana smiled in the satisfaction of the process.

The doorbell rang.

Dana ignored it and continued to concentrate on the wheel.

It rang a second time.

She glanced up, but all she could see was the top of a brown baseball cap in the upper windows of her front door. The letters "UPS" could clearly be seen on the cap, and Dana stopped the wheel, toweled off her hands, and rose to investigate.

She wasn't expecting a delivery today, but sometimes things came early or late. You never knew with United Parcel Service.

She approached the door and spoke from the far side.

"Can I help you?" asked Dana.

"UPS, ma'am," came the reply. "Delivery for Dana Kaminski?"

Dana glanced out the window and saw the large, brown UPS panel truck sitting in the driveway.

"Just a minute," said Dana.

Dana was not a paranoid woman, but she was no fool either. She unchained the lock and clicked open the deadbolt, opening the door to reveal not one, but three UPS delivery men standing on her front porch. All three had on the traditional UPS garb – brown short-sleeve shirt, brown shorts, and the brown UPS hat. One had a small package and the other had a clipboard.

"Sign here, ma'am," said the first UPS representative, holding the clipboard. He handed it over to Dana and extended a pen for her to use.

"Three of you on this route?" she inquired.

"Training day," said the second delivery man. She noticed that all three were lean and well built, even underneath the boring UPS uniforms.

"And no electronic delivery pad today?" she added, handing back the signed receipt.

"It's on the fritz," replied the first man, smiling, "- had to go the old-fashioned route."

The third man spoke up.

"Excuse me, ma'am, would you mind if I used your bathroom for a moment? We normally don't ask, but it's kind of an emergency."

She looked at the man, whose face had the expression of a man about to explode.

"Oh, all right," she said. "I wouldn't want you to have an accident."

She motioned the third delivery man past her and invited the other two into the foyer.

"First door on the left – down the hall," said Dana, talking over her shoulder. The third man disappeared.

The other two men waited patiently in the foyer. One turned to look out of the window, checking the street for any sign of traffic or movement. Dana thought it was a tad odd, but didn't show any concern at the moment.

"You make all of these?" said the first delivery man, pointing at the shelves in the living room and trying to maintain some small talk.

"Yes," said Dana, smiling. "It's my new obsession."

The third man returned from the hallway. He caught the first man's eye and gave a short nod. The first man nodded back his approval, then he turned to get the attention of the second delivery man, who was still looking out the window. He also nodded his head in acknowledgement.

The third man took two steps and came up behind Dana. With one arm, he quickly clamped down over Dana's mouth from behind. The first man moved in, blocking Dana's legs from instinctively rising and kicking out. Her eyes went suddenly wide, and she tried to scream, but no sound came out due to the hand-gag the third man had placed on her from behind.

She felt herself being pulled backwards into the third man's chest, then felt a sudden and sharp pain in her neck. The first man had already removed what looked like a large piece of gauze or padding from his pockets and was placing it up an around her shoulders. Dana's neck felt warm, and she was quickly becoming dizzy. Out of the corner of her eye, she caught the glint of a sharp, blood covered blade being removed from her neck and disappearing behind her. The first spout of blood was caught by the padding, and the first man was simply working on trying to catch the blood, not stop its flow. Dana tried to wriggle free in panic, but the first and third man now had all of her extremities in a firm lock. She was struggling, but no match for the UPS men's size and strength.

The second delivery man never turned to watch the proceedings. He kept his eyes on the yard and street in front of the house.

Soon, Dana's eyes glazed over and her body went limp. The first man released his grip and the third man began dragging Dana Kaminski's lifeless corpse towards the back yard.

The first man made sure there was no blood or other signs of the struggle left in the foyer. It was all very clean and efficient.

The third man returned a few minutes later.

"You're sure you've got it?" asked the first delivery man.

The third delivery man responded by reaching into his shirt pocket and removing a small rectangular plastic key.

On it were simple, large-block letters that read "NUMBER 1".

CHAPTER 14

Alan and Wendy made the turn-off into Burbank from Interstate 5 just as the sun was disappearing behind the buildings and trees to the West. The evening traffic on the "5" was, as always, a bear, and it took quite a while for Alan and Wendy to make their way into the Los Angeles suburb.

Dotted with small, 1950's style houses and palm tree lined streets, Burbank was not just a town known for television and movie studios. The quaint, tile roofed homes were a reminder of California's Spanish influence and style. Home prices also meant that only the affluent lived there, as even a 1,200- square foot home could go for almost $750,000 – even in today's depressed housing market.

Alan was following the GPS directions punched into the rental car's navigation system with the address supplied by Martin Boyle, and he soon turned onto the small back street where they would find the residence of Dana Kaminski.

As they approached the supplied street address, they noticed that a UPS van was backing out of the driveway. They slowed down their car and signaled, with the intent to turn into the driveway that the UPS van was backing out of, and Wendy took note that there were three UPS delivery men in the cab of the van, which she thought was unusual. While the driver kept watch on the road, the second man seemed to be staring directly at their rental car while the third man made eye contact with both Alan and Wendy.

The vehicles passed without incident, and Wendy watched the UPS van turn off of the side street and onto the main road as Alan parked in the driveway.

They got out and approached the house. Alan rang the doorbell as he and Wendy patiently waited on the front porch for an answer.

After a few seconds with no response, they rang the bell a second time - - -still nothing.

"She's got to be here," said Wendy. "The UPS guys just left and there's no package or note on the door."

"Ms. Kaminski?" said Alan, in a voice loud enough to be heard through the door. "Ms. Kaminski, are you in there? This is Agent Alan Silverman of the FBI. I'm here with Agent Wendy Tosca from the NSA. I wonder if we might have a word?"

Still nothing.

"Check around back," he said to Wendy, who moved towards the side of the house.

Alan continued to knock and call for Dana Kaminski.

Wendy turned the corner and saw a fence and gate that delineated the start of the Kaminski back yard. She approached the gate and knocked.

"Ms. Kaminski?" said Wendy. "Are you back there? This is Agent Wendy Tosca from the NSA. Can we speak with you for a moment?"

No response but silence.

She tried the gate, which was unlocked. Wendy slowly opened the gate and again called out as she entered the back yard. Rounding the corner to the back porch, she continued to call out.

"Ms. Kaminski?" said Wendy, in a louder voice. "Ms. Kaminski?"

She reached the back porch. There was a pottery wheel with a large cylinder still standing on its base. Wendy touched it, and noticed it was still very wet. There was also a cup of tea sitting on a chair next to the wheel. She put her hands around the cup – it was still warm.

She pulled her side-arm and made her way into the house.

"Alan?" she said, shouting towards the front door.

"Yeah?" he responded.

"Something's wrong here," she continued. "I'm coming towards you."

Wendy checked the hallway with a sweep of her weapon, then made her way towards the front door. She opened it and Alan entered. When he saw Wendy had pulled her weapon, he pulled his as well.

"Pottery is still fresh on the back porch," she whispered to Alan, who was now standing right beside her, "- cup of tea sitting on the table – it's still warm as well."

Alan nodded, then motioned that he would check the hall and back bedrooms. Wendy nodded and continued back towards the kitchen.

In a few moments, Wendy heard Alan call out from the back rooms.

"Clear," he said.

"Clear here as well," she responded. She re-holstered her weapon.

"Where is she?" said Alan as he joined Wendy, who was now standing next to the pottery wheel on the back porch. Wendy was taking a closer look at the fresh pottery.

"Don't know," said Wendy, "- but she can't be too far."

Alan looked into the back yard and noticed the kiln. The indicator light on its front was glowing orange, and smoke seemed to be seeping from the seal around the top of the device.

Alan poked Wendy and motioned towards the back yard.

They slowly approached the kiln. As they drew closer, they could easily tell now that it was running.

Wendy flicked a switch on the kiln's control panel and the indicator light extinguished. Up close, the heat radiating from the device was clearly evident. Alan grabbed some work gloves that were sitting on a concrete block next to the kiln. He put them on and motioned for Wendy to step back.

Alan lifted the lid. A hissing sound came from within, followed by a rushing cloud of steam. The smell was indescribable - - like a barbeque that had been left unattended. The scorching, stinging steam was laced with an unmistakable odor. It was the smell of burnt cloth and burnt flesh combined. It was the unique smell of death.

Wendy turned her head for a moment, trying to catch a gulp of fresh air. Alan hacked and coughed, retreating away from the steam and pulling his hands up over his nose and mouth.

They had found Dana Kaminski - - burning to cinders in her own makeshift crematorium.

CHAPTER 15

From the bedroom of his modern penthouse that overlooked Hong Kong's bustling business district, Vitaly Lukashenko surveyed the cityscape. At 6 feet two inches tall, the one hundred-eighty-five pound Ukrainian immigrant with gray eyes and long blonde locks (which he constantly kept tied up in a long pony-tail down his back) stood out in any crowd, no matter what city he was in. Vitaly was always perfectly groomed, from his manicured nails to his perfectly shaved face. He exuded a confidence and authority that made men – and women – gravitate towards him.

Driven by his own internal fire, Vitaly had grown up in the Crimean peninsula of the Ukraine, in a small village outside the southern city of Sevastopol. He excelled at everything he attempted – his schoolwork, athletics, and personal relationships. He graduated with honors and completed his secondary schooling abroad at Oxford. There he learned to speak fluent English, Spanish, and Chinese. He received a Master's degree in Computer Science and a secondary degree in Business Administration, which he used to found the Russian e-commerce company 'Utkonos'. Vitaly successfully sold his start-up company four years previously for well over a billion dollars.

He was a man who had been looking for direction - a man looking for a challenge.

Unfortunately, world events would shape Vitaly's future.

It had all started in 2013, when then Ukrainian President Viktor Vanukovych flatly rejected a deal that would have brought the Ukraine more closely aligned and integrated with the European Union. Mass protests erupted all over the country, which Vanukovych aggressively and mercilessly crushed with overwhelming force. Russia had backed Vanukovych while the United States had backed the protestors.

In February of 2014, Vanukovych and his government were overthrown by the protestors. Russia, sensing an opportunity and not wanting to lose its influence in the region, responded by invading Crimea, annexing its territory as part of Russia in March.

In April of that year, pro-separatist rebels began taking control of even more territory in eastern Ukraine, going as a far as shooting down a Malaysian Airliner and killing two-hundred-ninety-eight passengers. Again, Russia – sensing another opportunity, overtly invaded Eastern Ukraine during the confusion. They claimed it was to protect the citizens of the area who identified more with Russia than with the West.

The western powers responded with sanctions and threats, taking post-Cold War relations to an all-time low. Still – in the end, Russia had successfully annexed both Crimea and a large part of the eastern Ukraine without forceful opposition.   Citizens of the now-occupied territories who identified themselves more as part of the greater European Union than as a satellite of Russia felt abandoned and betrayed.

Vitaly Lukashenko was just angry.

His homeland had been overrun – and the world had just stood by and watched. They let it happen – and did nothing. Vitaly's mother had been killed in the regional fighting. His boyhood home had been destroyed by government forces. Thousands had been displaced in the region. Reports of atrocities surfaced all over the internet.

The powers of the West simply waved their fists at the Russians, shouting threats and enacting economic sanctions, but in the end, the land was taken – probably for good.

Vitaly knew that.

His purpose was clear. He would not be deterred. He would make them all pay for their actions. The Russians -- and the West. He would show them what real power was.

He closed his eyes and sighed, trying to calm his soul.

The phone rang, interrupting his peace. He hit a button on the console, enabling the speaker-phone.

"Yes?" he said, curtly.

"Sir, Phase Three of the collection process had just successfully completed," said a Chinese voice over the speaker. It was Wu Li Chang, calling from the Operations Center with his morning briefing.

"Excellent," said Vitaly, "- and 'Apokalypsis'?"

"Still on schedule," replied Wu Li.

Vitaly closed his eyes and took another deep breath in satisfaction.

"We may have another development," said Wu Li.

Vitaly opened one eye and glanced over towards the phone. "Problems?"

"Possibly," said Wu Li. "During the Phase Three extraction, our team encountered some unexpected visitors at the site."

"Have they been identified?" asked Vitaly.

"We traced the rental car records. The car was rented to an agent Alan Silverman of the FBI cyber-crimes unit. He was also with an agent from the NSA – a Miss Wendy

Tosca.   It does not seem like a coincidence that they were there."

"It wasn't," said Vitaly. "Was our team compromised?"

"No," said Wu Li. "The extraction completed – as planned. "

Vitaly stood in silence for a moment. Eventual knowledge and investigations by worldwide governments were expected, but the American presence had developed more quickly than he had anticipated.

"Your orders, sir?" asked Wu Li.

Vitaly stared out at the Hong Kong skyline for another few moments.

"Have the agents monitored," said Vitaly. "If they show up at any of the other extraction points or interfere with any aspect of the operation, alert me at once."

"As you wish," said Wu Li. The phone was hung up from the other end.

Vitaly thumbed the speaker phone off. He wasn't worried. Though unexpected, the government agents would fumble around, following established procedures. It would be all over before they even had any real idea of what was going on – and besides - there was no way they could do anything to prevent it.

He smiled at the view one last time and went into the bathroom for a nice hot shower. It was going to be a busy day.

CHAPTER 16

"Whatcha thinking about?" said Wendy, looking over at Alan, who was seated next to her.

After turning over the crime scene at the home of Dana Kaminski to local law enforcement and catching the red-eye flight from Los Angeles back to Washington D.C., Alan was now leaned up against the window of the east bound United Airlines flight with his eyes shut. His legs were cramped and he was grumpy.

"I was thinking about getting some sleep," said Alan, a bit annoyed. "It's been quite a long day."

"How can you sleep?" said Wendy.

"I generally shut my eyes – and shut my mouth," he replied. His eyes were still closed and he was trying to ignore Wendy, but it wasn't working.

"Do you think Kaminski's key-card was lost in the kiln?" she asked.

"Doubtful," said Alan. It was clear he wasn't going to get any shut-eye – at least not for a while. He straightened up in his seat and opened the soda sitting on his tray table.

"I'd say our UPS boys probably have it on them," continued Alan. They had checked with the local UPS office. There was no scheduled delivery for the address that day – and they confirmed they never sent drivers out in three-man teams. "Either way, I think we have to assume that her key-card is gone. If they need five out of seven to reset the system and we've got three missing keys, I'd say we had a problem in any case."

"Did you get the list of remaining key-card holders from Martin?" she asked.

"Yes," said Alan. "They've all checked in for this week, but I called back to the office and filled them in. Supposedly, they are going to send out some agents to collect them – the TCRs AND their cards - for their own safety."

"Where else did they have to go?" she asked.

"I'll say one thing for ICANN," said Alan. " – they like to keep it interesting. They've got key holders in Canada, China, the Czech Republic, and Burkina Faso."

"Where in the world is Burkina Faso?" said Wendy.

"Well it sure isn't in Ohio," said Alan. "Couldn't tell you – but they have a guy there, I guess."

"We still don't have a clue as to how these DNS outages are happening," said Wendy. She opened her small bag of in-flight peanuts and was munching away.

"I have a feeling we'll get another chance to look at the logs of another outage in the near future, don't you?" said Alan.

Wendy was silent for a few moments, occasionally tossing a peanut into her mouth. Alan just stared at her.

"Well, Jumbo, if you're going to be quiet for a while, I'm going to try to catch some Z's - if you don't mind" said Alan, who started to lean his head back up against the bulkhead.

"I think I may know of someone who can help us," said Wendy.

"I'm all ears, and could you please chew with your mouth shut?" said Alan.

"Sweet dreams, Rip Van Winkle," she said, smiling. "I'll tell you when we land."

"Fine," said Alan, closing his eyes. "Now – shut up."

Wendy pulled out the in-flight magazine and tried to read for a bit. She suddenly realized that she was worn out as well.

In five minutes she was out like a light, her head leaning on Alan's shoulder.

CHAPTER 17

It had been a productive morning for Frank Alvis. From his small apartment in downtown Pittsburgh, there was nothing in the material world Frank couldn't have or obtain, as long as he had a laptop and a good internet connection. Programming takes a certain mindset, and Frank certainly had it. He had never done well in his other subjects at school. In truth, he had barely graduated from high school. Even so, his math and computer teachers recognized a stroke of genius hidden somewhere inside that bulky, overweight frame. His ability to almost sense how to break down and write code, as well as his understanding of advanced mathematics and complex subjects such as network topology and machine code were almost savant-like. His teachers had all been encouraging, trying to convince him to apply to colleges or technical schools in order to continue to advance his math and computer knowledge.

Frank; however, was never concerned about what other people thought. It reflected in both his attitude towards mainstream society and also in his appearance. He was overweight, his skin was bad, and he had long, unkempt hair and a straggly beard. His days were spent slumped over his multiple computer screens, rarely taking a break to shower or devote any time whatsoever to personal hygiene.

His apartment was also a mess. Empty take-out boxes littered the couches and floor, there were dishes piled high in the sink, and dirty clothes were strewn about the apartment.

None of that mattered to Frank. In the computer world, he was only motivated by the excitement of the chase. The quest to obtain the seemingly unobtainable. Getting access to the inaccessible.

Frank was born to be a hacker – and he was a damn good one.

His online moniker was 'Tron007', and in the online world, the name 'Tron007' was both revered and feared. Even Fortune 500 companies and their IT departments were aware of him. If 'Tron007' wanted to get into your system, it was pretty much assured that 'Tron007' was going to get into your system - - end of story. There were actually teams of people in both government agencies and in the commercial sector that were dedicated to trying to come up with "Tron007-proof" systems.

Frank was a legend - - and he knew it.

This morning, Frank's disk drives and printers had been busy. So far he had obtained season tickets for the Penguins hockey team, was now an American Airlines Executive Club Premiere member (with all of its perks), and he had successfully downloaded all three seasons of HBO's 'Game of Thrones' TV series.

He was now doing some comparison shopping on the Consumer Reports website. Frank was in the mood for a big screen TV, and of course, he wanted the best. Never mind the fact that he wouldn't be paying for it when he decided to purchase it later on today. There were ways around that. Amazon had everything, and as long as they didn't have any more annoying outages (like they had experienced recently), there would be a delivery waiting at his door the following afternoon.

He was interrupted by a knock at his door. Frank didn't have many friends, and certainly not in Pittsburgh, so he ignored it. Probably a pollster or Seventh-Day Adventist looking to spread the good word. He took a slug of his Red Bull energy drink and continued to peruse the Consumer Reports ratings.

A second knock came, this one stronger and more urgent. Whoever it was, they were certainly persistent. He stopped typing, just in case they could somehow hear his keystrokes on the other side of the door.

After a few silent seconds, he resumed his browsing.

That's when he heard a key being inserted into his lock and the tumblers turning. He swiveled around in his desk chair and was preparing to get up when the door opened.

It was Wendy Tosca, her sidearm drawn and at the ready. Alan was close behind her. Frank raised his hands to show he was unarmed.

"Don't shoot, don't shoot!" yelled out Frank. "Wendy, it's just me."

Wendy scanned the room and then dropped her sidearm, re-holstering it at her side.

"Frank, why aren't you answering the door?" she said, a bit annoyed at him. She came further into the room as she spoke to him. Alan closed the door behind them both.

"Good lord, Frank, have you ever thought about a 'Febreze'?", said Wendy, waving her hand over her nose in disgust. She scanned the room again, this time shaking her head at its condition. "You could choke a goat in here."

"I like it the way I like it," Frank said, not getting up from his chair, "- it doesn't bother me."

"That's because you're a slob," said Wendy. She walked over to a chair in the living room and threw some dirty laundry off of its seat and onto the floor. She brushed the cushions with her hand and sat down.

"How have you been, Frank?" said Wendy, gingerly settling into the chair.

"Fine," said Frank. He was keeping his eyes on Alan, who was looking over the room and had wandered into the kitchen. "Who's the stiff?"

"Oh, him?" said Wendy. "You'll like him, Frank – he's FBI."

Frank's face suddenly dropped and he seemed concerned. Wendy read it instantly.

"Stop worrying, Frank," said Wendy. "If we would have wanted to arrest you, we'd have done it by now. We just want to talk to you."

Frank relaxed a bit, but still seemed wary. Alan was making his way out of the kitchen.

"Alan," Wendy said, "- I'd like you to meet Frank Alvis." She motioned towards the chair. "Frank, this is Alan Silverman – he's with the FBI's cyber-crime division."

Frank tensed up again as Alan extended his hand. Frank just stared at it and didn't offer his in return. After a few seconds, Alan shrugged and removed his offer to shake hands.

"What can I do for you?" said Frank, staring at Alan.

"Oh, I think it's what you can do for US, Frank," said Wendy. "Alan, let me tell you a little about Frank – grab a seat," she said, motioning towards the couch in the room.

"Is it safe?" said Alan, eyeing the piece of furniture that was strewn with empty pizza boxes and empty energy drink cans.

"Nothing a little penicillin won't cure," said Wendy, glancing over at Frank. Frank was not amused.

Alan cleared off a space and sat down.

"Now about big boy over here," said Wendy, looking back over at Frank, "– our friend Frank is a bit of a computer genius."

Frank blushed a little at the compliment and stared at the floor, smiling a little to himself. Secretly, he loved hearing people talk about him and his accomplishments. He knew Wendy was about to lay out his resume for the visitor.

"You see, Frank likes to snoop around other people's systems. You know, the phone company, corporate websites – that sort of thing. He also likes to take things without paying for them."

Frank was still staring at the floor, but his smile had faded away.

"I don't steal from people," Frank explained. "I take from companies – it doesn't hurt anyone."

"Quiet, Robin Hood," said Wendy, scolding Frank, "– the adults are talking."

"So one day," Wendy continued, "- old Frank here gets bored and hacks into the Pentagon's secure website. Now he's really stepped into it, which is how I met him."

"And why isn't Frank rotting away in Leavenworth or Gitmo right now?" asked Alan.

"Good question," said Wendy. "You see, Frank possesses a very special set of skills - -skills which the NSA doesn't readily have."

"Ahhh," said Alan. "You needed a good hacker."

Wendy nodded her head. "Frank here is a bit of a big deal in the online world – goes by the name of – what is it Frank – 'Tron007'?"

Frank nodded from his seat.

"Well, the NSA uses the infamous 'Tron007' here for little jobs from time to time," said Wendy.

"You mean 'black bag' stuff," said Alan.

"Oh, it's usually not that exciting," said Wendy, "- but nevertheless, we have an agreement. Frank does what we ask of him, when we ask of him – and in exchange, he gets to keep living here in the lap of luxury."

"So you've blackmailed him," said Alan.

"I wouldn't call it that," said Wendy. "It's a business arrangement – and I'm sort of his business manager, isn't that right, Frank?"

Frank continued to stare at the floor, but nodded his head in agreement.

"What about his other activities?" said Alan. "Aren't you worried Frank is going to hack you personally - - or the NSA?"

"If he does, he knows we'll lock him up and throw away the key," said Wendy, staring at Frank. "We let him do his thing – we don't really care if he steals from corporations and what not – just as long as he doesn't screw with us."

"I won't," said Frank. "Wendy, you know I won't." Frank had seen enough online videos of treatment at "government" prisons. The mere thought of being locked up tight in "regular" prison scared Frank. His mind had also created even worse horrors just thinking about what would be in store for him if the government wanted him gone.

"Good man," said Wendy, " - - now, down to business. I assume you've heard about the recent outages for companies like Amazon. "

Frank perked up a bit.

"Yeah," said Frank. "What about them?"

"The Amazon thing and many of these other outages are related," said Alan. "Someone crushed their DNS resolution – temporarily. We don't know how they did it."

"And we want you to do some snooping and find out for us," continued Wendy, jumping into the explanation. "You think you can do that?"

A puzzle - - the kind of computer puzzle that Frank liked. His mind was already spinning in a hundred directions, recalling what he knew about DNS and IP resolution.

"Sure," said Frank. He was now in a much better mood. "You have any logs I can look at?"

"We can get them for you," said Alan. "What's his clearance level?" he asked, looking towards Wendy.

"Whatever he needs," said Wendy.

"We'll have to get the files to him somehow," said Alan.

"And we need a quick turnaround on this, Frank," added Wendy. "We don't know how or why these outages are happening – and we think more are on the way."

Now it was Frank's turn. "Hold on," he said.

He swiveled around in his chair and began looking for something to write with. He found a pen and scribbled a few lines onto a piece of paper, tore it off, and gave it to Alan.

"What's this?" said Alan. The paper had several IP addresses scrawled on it.

"You put the files on the server at that location – I'll do the rest," said Frank.

"Where the hell is this at?" asked Alan.

"It's one of the FBI secure servers in your building back in D.C.," said Frank, smiling again.

Alan looked over at Wendy in shock. Wendy just smiled a proud smile.

"I told you he was a bad boy," said Wendy.

CHAPTER 18

At Symantec Headquarters, it was late in the evening and almost everyone had left the office for the day.

One person left was Garrett Hamilton.

He had been killing time for the last hour, playing solitaire on his office laptop, patiently waiting for the last programmers on the floor to leave.

Maria Chung moved past Garrett's open office door and stopped short.

"You still here, Garrett?" she asked from the doorway.

Garrett's mind was wandering all over the place. He barely realized someone was talking to him.

"What?" he said, his mind now registering the voice in the doorway. He looked up from his laptop screen to a smiling Maria, who was still in the doorway and waiting for an answer.

"Late night for management," she added, chuckling a bit.

"Oh," said Garrett   now focusing in on the conversation, "- yeah – um – always paperwork to catch up on," he added in.

"Well, don't work too hard," said Maria. "See you tomorrow," she added turning to go down the hall.

"Right – see you," he responded.

From his desk, Garrett watched Maria walk down the hall to the lobby area, where she boarded an elevator and disappeared.

He then rose and made one cursory lap of the office cubicle areas. He wanted to make sure that there was really no one left. He didn't want to be disturbed while completing the task at hand.

He stopped in the break room on his way back and got another cup of coffee. His hands were shaking as he poured it. Garrett took a deep breath. He needed to calm down.

He slowly walked back towards his office and thought about the events of the past few weeks. When had he been contacted – over a year ago now?

Garrett remembered that first face-to-face meeting. It had been after months of email messages. He couldn't even remember how the subject of Crimea and the Ukraine had come up, but soon there were passionate discussions about patriotism, politics, and most importantly, family. Garrett's relatives on his mother's side were Crimean, and they had lost everything in the recent turmoil. He wanted to go there to help, but there was - of course - a recommended travel ban to the area instituted by the U.S. State department. The U.S.

Government feared for American lives, but didn't seem to care about the lives that were left in Ukraine and Crimea - - lives that had been torn apart from the unrest and fighting. It was obvious to Garrett - just as it had been to his email confidant - that no one cared.

Soon, jobs and career came up, and the email stranger turned out to be a fellow IT professional. He was going to be in the area — and could they meet?

"Why not?" thought Garrett.

The stranger had introduced himself as Viktor Lorsov. He had a commanding presence — tall, long blonde hair swept back in a ponytail, and the strangest grey eyes. It was as if they looked straight Garrett to his very soul.

Soon, a plan was introduced to Garrett. Viktor wanted a job done, and he was willing to pay handsomely for it. Ten million dollars — for ten minute's work. Viktor had stated that the money would be deposited in escrow in a numbered Swiss bank account. That way, no one would know that the transaction had even occurred. The money would be accessible wherever and whenever Garrett needed it. He could even use it to help his Ukrainian relatives.

"Family is everything," Viktor had told him. "All of this," he motioned around the coffee shop, "- these are just things. Things can be replaced."

Viktor was powerful and persuasive, but Garrett also realized what he was asking.

Viktor wanted a subroutine embedded into Symantec's antivirus code. Viktor would take care of everything. Garrett just had to continue on with his daily routine and do his job as he normally would. At some point, he would be contacted. Then he would insert the provided code into the next Norton update and ensure it was sent out in the next code release.

"What's the subroutine do?" asked Garrett.

"It's a wake-up call," said Viktor. "The world will realize what's important – like you and I understand."

It had all made sense at the time, Garrett thought. He had nodded his head slowly in agreement.

Vitkor reached across the table to shake Garrett's hand.

"How will I know when you want this done?" asked Garrett.

"You'll receive a code word," said Viktor.

"Which is?" asked Garrett.

Viktor stared straight at Garrett, speaking slowly and carefully.

"'Apokalypsis'," said Viktor.

CHAPTER 19

Garrett had made it back to his office. He sat in his chair, and typed in access to a secure server that had been provided to him. His office was cool, but he was sweating.

On the screen, in a single file folder was a small file. It was simply titled "ABC.zip".

He copied the file, then switched his access over to the Symantec project server. He brought up the latest project files his team had been diligently working on over the last three weeks. The latest updates to the Norton Anti-Virus Suite were being pushed out to computers all over the very next morning at 07:00.

He pasted in the code and saved the update file.

The newest Norton release now had twenty-eight updates instead of twenty-seven for its next software push, but one update was known only to a specific system architect.

Garrett looked out into the hallway, half expecting at any moment for a policeman or a team of federal agents to come rushing out of the elevator and down the hall towards his office – guns drawn.

No one came. The elevator doors remained closed and silent.

Garrett relaxed a bit. It was done. He signed back onto the secure server and typed in the word "Apokalypsis" at the command prompt.

The screen stayed blank for a few moments – then the words "transfer complete" along with a twelve digit code number – the link to a numbered Swiss bank account – appeared on the screen.

He jotted down the code number and signed off of the secure connection. He sat back in his chair and allowed himself a small smile.

Garrett Hamilton had just become a multi-millionaire.

He was shaking again.

CHAPTER 20

The morning hadn't been a great one for Alan Silverman. He was back at his desk in "the cage" at the FBI's Cyber-Crime Division Main office at FBI headquarters in Washington, D.C. He had spent the morning in meetings, trying to juggle his case load. Even though had had pounded three Advil an hour before, his head was aching. The DNS problem was becoming more and more ominous, but there were still other cases that demanded his attention.

He had just slumped into his desk chair after returning from the cafeteria. He tossed a half-eaten BLT onto a stack of papers on his desk, closed his eyes, and rubbed his temples, trying to drown out the noise and distractions from the other cubicles around him.

"Bad morning?" said Wendy, sticking her head into Alan's cubicle. She almost didn't want to disturb him, he looked so out of sorts.

"Meetings," murmured Alan, still not opening his eyes. He blew out a giant puff of air and ran his hands through his hair. "I hate meetings."

He opened his eyes and motioned for her to come in. Wendy sat down in the empty visitor's chair in Alan's cube.

"Can I interest you in some lunch?" said Alan. He pointed at the half eaten sandwich on his desk.

"Uhhh, thanks — but no thanks," said Wendy, eyeing the sandwich warily. "I've got some news for you on our magical key-card holders."

"Please tell me some good news," he said, turning towards her, "- I could use some this morning."

"Well, it's not all roses and chocolate, I'm afraid," she said. "The key holders in Canada and the Czech Republic have been located and secured in a safe location — along with their key-cards."

"That's a start," said Alan. "What about the ones in China and Burkina Faso?" he added.

"We've made voice contact with the holder in Burkina Faso," said Wendy, "- oh, by the way - that's in West Africa — I know you were interested," she added.

"Thanks, but I had looked it up," said Alan, shooting Wendy a sarcastic grin. "Why just voice contact?"

"The infrastructure there isn't exactly state of the art," Wendy added. "Plus, the politics there are a bit murky — we have to go through intermediaries. It's not like we can just send a Blackhawk helicopter in there to swoop down and pick this guy up."

"When do they think they'll have him?" asked Alan.

"Twenty-four hours, at the most," said Wendy.

"Well, that's three out of the four remaining," said Alan. "What about the China holder?"

"No luck yet," said Wendy.

"That's bad," said Alan, "- you're only allowed to tell me good news." His head was throbbing again.

"Buck-up, cowboy," said Wendy. "That's as good as it gets – for now." She rose to leave. "I'll keep you posted," she said, disappearing down the hall.

"Wonderful," said Alan to his empty cubicle. He grabbed his half eaten BLT and tossed it into the garbage, then swiveled around in his chair and got back to work.

CHAPTER 21

Although Vitaly Lukashenko was a confidant man, he was not necessarily a patient one.

Vitaly was sitting in his high-backed swivel chair which overlooked his Data Operations Center in Hong Kong. He was watching the monitors attached to the far wall, his back to the actual Operations floor, but wasn't focused on any of them. A half-finished cigarette rested comfortably in his hand, the smoke tracing a lazy line up towards the ceiling before dissipating.

Vitaly was waiting on an update from Wu Li Chang, his trusted lieutenant and 2nd in command of this operation.

Wu Li was late – and Wu Li was never late.

In a few more moments, Vitaly heard the "tap-tap" of Wu Li's shoes as they quickly ascended the metal steps towards the overlook where Vitaly was stationed. He heard Wu Li trying to catch his breath as he waited for acknowledgement across Vitaly's desk. Vitlay didn't turn his chair around.

"You're late," said Vitaly, with more than a little venom in his voice.

"My apologies," said Wu Li, his head was bowed in submission.

Vitaly slowly turned the chair around to face Wu.

"Well," said Vitaly, "- explain yourself."

"It's our collection operation," he said, regaining his composure. "The FBI and NSA have been sending out agents."

Vitaly was now clearly annoyed. He crushed out the cigarette in an ashtray on his desk and sat up straighter in his chair.

"And?" said Vitaly. He was now focused completely on Wu Li and his words. Vitaly was giving Wu Li a hateful stare. Wu Li again dropped his gaze to the floor in front of the desk.

"The key holders in both Canada and the Czech Republic have been alerted and picked up by the American authorities," said Wu.

Vitaly slammed his hand down on the desk and cursed under his breath. It was that FBI and NSA agent that had been encountered in the American extraction operation – it had to be. They were putting the pieces together. He turned his chair around – away from Wu Li – in disgust.

Wu Li did not move. He simply waited.

"Burkina Faso?" said the voice from the chair.

"Still out there," said Wu Li. "The Americans haven't located that target as of yet, and we hadn't activated that portion of our extraction operation, either. It was going to be the last one – and only if we needed it."

"It's obvious we don't now," said Vitaly. "Cancel that portion of the operation. We'll have enough keys to proceed."

"Our contact from Symantec has successfully uploaded our code into the next Norton release," said Wu Li, hoping that some good news would improve his boss's mood.

"Good," said Vitaly. He smiled to himself. That Symantec coder – what was his name – Garrett? He'd been so easily to manipulate. Americans – they were all the same – wave some currency under their noses and one could get them to do anything.

Vitaly could sense that Wu Li had not left yet. He swiveled his chair around, wiping the smile off of his face and giving a serious glance at Wu Li, who he was still disappointed with for being late.

"You have something else?" asked Vitaly.

"Yes," said Wu Li. He dropped his gaze again. "I was followed this morning. That's why I was late."

Vitaly seemed surprised. "Are you sure?"

"Positive," said Wu Li. "I've also received several phone calls from an unknown number to my house phone. I was ignoring them, but today, a pair of men were following me as I came here."

Vitaly was again annoyed at Wu Li.

"So you continued to come in?" said Vitaly. His anger was rising.

"I lost them," assured Wu Li holding his hands out in reassurance.

"How can you be sure?" said Vitaly.

"I'm sure," said Wu Li. "I've been on and off the subway multiple times. Plus, I've been in large, crowded places - like the public market - all over town. I assure you, I lost them."

"You had better be," said Vitaly. "I will not stand for losing another key-card. I will hold you personally responsible."

"Oh, it's still safe," said Wu Li.

He reached into his back pocket and pulled out a small, gray key-card. It was blank except for some large, black lettering on one side that read simply "NUMBER 5".

Wu Li Chang was the China key-card holder.

"Give it to me," demanded Vitaly. "I can't afford to let you hold it any longer."

"As you wish," said Wu Li. He bowed his head and formally presented the card with both hands across the desk. Vitaly quickly swiped it out of his hand and laid it on the desk in front of him.

"Our visitors from the FBI an NSA who were encountered in our American extraction," said Vitaly, "– are they still being monitored?"

"Yes sir," said Wu Li. He was a bit embarrassed now. His honor had been called into question by being forced to turn over his key-card.

"Eliminate them – as soon as possible," said Vitaly. "I don't want any more surprises, Wu."

"Yes sir," said Wu Li, again. He bowed and left the elevated office, hurrying down the stairs. He would regain his honor – and the trust of his employer.

Vitaly turned back around in his chair towards the monitors. He was still angry. This was why he relied only on himself for success. Still, things were still progressing – even with Wu Li's recent bad news.

Soon, "Apokalypsis" would be unleashed, and he would sit back and joyfully watch the world's economies burn.

He smiled again to himself and lit another cigarette.

CHAPTER 22

Frank Alvis was a little paranoid.

Knowing what he knew about the internet and computers, he made a conscious effort not to say too much over a phone line. All Wendy had gotten out of him was "I've got something to show you," on her NSA office phone line.

Now she and Alan were on another plane, headed back to Pittsburgh.

"For someone with literally no field experience, you sure are racking up the miles," she chided Alan, who was again sitting next to her. Alan just rolled his eyes and returned to the crossword puzzle he was working on from the morning paper.

"I don't see why this tub just can't tell us his news over the phone," said Alan. "If anyone's listening, it's just our guys."

"Sometimes you have to play along," said Wendy. "Besides, if Frank contacted us, he's definitely got something important to share, so just relax."

"I'd be relaxing if I were in front of that curtain," said Alan, pointing at the flimsy barrier that separated the plane's coach section from business class.

"Government cutbacks" said Wendy, shrugging her shoulders. "Besides, in the end, you pay for it anyway – with taxes."

"Easy Senator," said Alan. "It's just hard to relax when one's legs are folded up like a pretzel."

In about an hour, they found themselves back at the door of Frank's dirty apartment. Wendy knocked.

"What do you want?" came the reply from the other side.

"You called us, remember?" said Wendy.

"Oh, it's you," said Frank. He unlocked the door and let them come in. The apartment was still a complete mess – only more so - if that was possible.

"I see you've had the maids in," said Alan, cracking a joke.

"Nice, 'G-Man'," said Frank.

"I assume this is important," said Wendy, getting them back on track.

"It is," said Frank. "Have a seat and I'll show you."

Frank sat back down at his desk, three large monitors facing him. Wendy threw some old laundry off of a spare chair, pulled it up next to Frank, and sat down. Alan looked around and finding no open seats, eventually realized he'd be standing.

"It's actually pretty cool, what they've done here," said Frank, tapping on his keyboard and pulling up some files.

"You found out what was causing the DNS outages?" said Alan. He reluctantly removed a pair of reading glasses from his pocket and put them on, trying to bring Frank's monitors into focus.

"Are they related?" asked Wendy.

"Yup," said Frank. "At least the two you gave me access to are – I'm gonna assume the others were done the same way."

"What did you find?" said Alan.

"Right here," said Frank, pointing to a line in the system log. "It looks like an ordinary system message – the thing is - the software that would have generated this message isn't on this system."

"You sure?" said Alan, squinting to see the screen.

"Very," said Frank, "- my guess is that whoever did this "piggy-backed" some code in on something else – some sort of download. The program masked the DNS resolution table, then once it was done, it repaired itself and wrote over the malicious code."

"To cover its tracks?" said Wendy.

"Exactly," said Frank. He was excited now, clearly in his element. "I'd say you've gotten off lucky so far."

"And why is that?" asked Alan.

"Because," Frank continued, "- whoever is doing this WANTED it to get fixed. They included the code to unmask the DNS resolution table. If they wished, they could have just destroyed the table all together, which would have caused all kinds of problems."

Alan and Wendy looked at each other. This confirmed the hypothesis that Martin Boyle had laid out for them at ICANN.

"So if the DNS resolution table is destroyed, the IP addresses can't be resolved and the hardware is blind," said Alan, still looking at Wendy - who was nodding her head in agreement.

"Hey, that's pretty good," said Frank, "- who told you about that?"

"You're just confirming a hypothesis we were toying around with," said Wendy, turning her gaze back at the screen.

"Can you tell where this code came from or on what program it rode in on?" asked Alan.

"That will take some time to completely confirm," said Frank, "- but I can tell you what *country* I'm pretty sure it came from," he added.

"I'm listening," said Wendy.

"This fake system code line," said Frank, "- it's a message from of a "knock- off" program."

"What's a "knock-off" program?" asked Alan.

"Pirate code," said Frank. "A foreign competitor steals code from some Fortune 500 company and changes it up a bit, just to try and avoid any patent infringement or legal trouble. Some companies are more blatant than others."

"And this code?" said Alan. "You can tell where it's from?"

"Oh yeah," said Frank. "This is Chinese – all the way. Specifically, it matches the type of pirate code I've seen a few times coming out of Hong Kong."

"Can you tell what program it may have come from?" said Wendy.

"Yup," said Frank, who was clearly enjoying being the star of the show.

"And?" said Alan.

"Anti-virus software," said Frank. "It's a knock off of Symantec's Norton Anti-Virus Suite."

Alan and Wendy looked at each other again – dumbfounded. Frank sat back in his chair and folded his arms in satisfaction.

"Nobody messes with 'Tron007'", said Wendy smiling at Frank. She leaned over and gave him a quick kiss on the cheek.

Frank's smile grew twice as wide.

CHAPTER 23

Danny Zhu sat in his car parked along the curb of a Hong Kong street, disgusted at himself. It had been a terrible morning.

He and his partner, Brian Tan, had been assigned by the CIA's Station "H" in Hong Kong to find and pick up a person of interest - -routine stuff. Except for one thing – there had been specific instructions to bring in their target along with some sort of key-card he was supposedly carrying. Whatever – it was just another pick-up job.

The man in question, Wu Li Chang, seemed mild mannered enough by his background check. Some computer nerd, Danny had remembered. It should have been simple, but it was turning out to be anything but.

Somehow, this guy picked up on the fact that he was being followed and it spooked him. He bolted, and had led Danny and Brian on a merry chase all over Hong Kong that morning. Rather than create a scene and try to capture him in public, the agents had decided to let Wu Li cool off. They had seen this before. Let your mark calm down, get comfortable – they would return to their normal routine soon enough.

Danny was sure they would catch up to their target later on that day – most likely after work. He and Brian had parked down the street from Wu Li's apartment, far enough from the residence as to not raise any suspicions, but close enough to see whenever their target returned.

They had settled in for a lengthy wait. Brian was out grabbing them some food, and Danny was closely watching the entire block for any sign of their man. He had even adjusted his side and rear-view mirrors so they were pointed at the street behind him. It was a continuous cycle on the stake-out. Check ahead – scan the side mirrors – check the rear-view - hour after hour. It was why Danny and Brian took turns being "on point". It took more discipline to keep up the visual scanning than it sounded like.

He spotted Brian coming lazily up the street - take out containers in hand, as well as a cardboard drink caddy.

Brian surveyed the street one last time for anything suspicious himself before sliding into the passenger seat of the surveillance car.

"What did you get?" said Danny, still concentrating on his street scans.

"Some stir-fry chicken, rice, and steamed pork buns," said Brian. He was pulling out various cartons and placing them around the passenger seat. He handed a hot tea across the console to Danny.

"Those pork buns are gonna make you sleepy," Danny warned Brian. "They always do."

"Shut-up, man," said Brian. "What do you care? You get a break in a few – it's me who has to worry about it."

Danny took a sip of his hot tea and chuckled.

Brian greedily gulped down about six pork buns and washed it down with some hot tea of his own.

"I'm ready for the hand-off, whenever you are," he said to Danny as he wiped his mouth off on his sleeve.

Danny gave one final cursory sweep of the street and his mirrors.

"All yours," he said. He then opened the box with the stir fry chicken and rice and began to eat with the supplied chopsticks.

Brian picked up right where Danny had left off. Now he was concentrating on the street, performing a full visual sweep of the area about every twenty to thirty seconds.

Danny hadn't taken more than two bites of his food when he was startled by Brian, who touched him on the shoulder.

"Heads up," said Brian. "There's our man now – ten-o'clock."

Danny dropped his chopsticks into the chicken carton and looked in the direction supplied by Brian.

Wu Li had just rounded the corner down the street from his apartment and was making his way towards them. He did not seem hurried or anxious, as he had been all morning when he had Danny and Brian on the run.

Danny glanced at the clock in the car. It was 2:17 PM. Maybe Wu Li was coming home for a late lunch - or had forgotten something from earlier. Danny hadn't expected to see him this soon.

They waited until Wu had ascended the short flight of steps to his building's entrance and had fully entered. Danny and Brian both left their lunches and tea and exited the car separately, so they would not arouse any suspicion. Brian lazily made his way down the street, stopping at a newsstand to casually look at some magazines. Danny walked past the building all together, giving an uninterested glance into the apartment building's foyer. No sign of Wu Li, which meant he had gone up to his apartment.

Danny slowly circled back around and gave a short nod to Brian. They both then made their way up the small staircase to Wu's apartment and entered, Danny holding the door for Brian as he took one last look at the streetscape for anything unusual.

Everything was quiet and normal.

Danny and Brian got in the elevator and punched in Wu Li's floor. He lived on the seventeenth floor - probably a good view of the city from up there. They both checked that their side-arms were loaded and still well concealed.

The door slid open on seventeen and Danny peered carefully around the corner.

Nothing.

They carefully and quietly made their way down the hall to apartment #1714, Wu Li Chang's address.

Danny stood off to one side, out of the doorway while Brian knocked.

There was a slight pause.

"Who is it?" came the reply from behind the door.

"Mr. Chang?" said Brian. "I'm Officer Tan from the Hong Kong police department." This was a standard greeting - stating that one was an agent from the CIA or NSA tended to freak people out from the get-go.

"Is there a problem?" came the voice from behind the door.

"No sir," said Brian. "I just need to speak with you for a moment – may I come in?"

"One second," said the voice.

In less than that Brian and Danny heard the deadbolt turning, and the door opened partway. Wu Li peered around the corner. Brian immediately and almost imperceptibly placed his foot in the door jam, so Wu Li would not be able to shut it on them.

Wu Li saw that there were now two officers in his doorway - officers with no police uniforms on. His face dropped. Brain immediately sensed it and now had one hand on the door (in addition to his foot) to keep it from closing. His other had reached for his badge. Danny was also pulling his. They both flashed them to Wu Li, who took careful note of them.

"Actually, Mr. Chang," said Brian, "we're from the CIA field office here in Hong Kong."

Wu Li looked surprised, then glanced down at the badges again. Both confirmed they were from the CIA.

"We just need to talk to you for a few moments," added in Danny. "There's nothing to be alarmed about. May we come in?"

Wu Li looked skeptical, but relented, backing away from the door as he opened it. Brian and Danny were both inside now and had shut the door behind them.

"What's this all about?" asked Wu. He walked the agents down the hall towards his living room area. They passed an open door on the left. The room behind it was dark. Danny passed by it and was followed by Brian. Brian assumed it was Wu Li's bedroom. He had taken a half-hearted glance at it when his attention was drawn directly ahead.

Wu Li was already standing in the small living room, looking back towards the hall. As Danny entered, a darkly dressed figure exploded from the corner of the room and attacked Danny. They had tumbled down onto the floor, the stranger quickly gaining the upper hand on Danny due to the surprise and unexpectedness of the attack.

Brian had just leaned forward to race into the room when he felt a small cord slip over his head and tighten around his neck. He was thrust backwards, almost off of his heels, as a second figure emerged from the room on the left side of the hall and took him by surprise as well.

Brian tried to step back and correct his balance, but his assailant was a professional. For every move attempted by Brian to escape, his attacker had a counter-move – all the while tightening his grip on Brian's throat.

Brian could see it was all over for Danny. His assailant had plunged a small commando-style dagger into his ribs, and Danny had gone limp and slumped to the floor.

All the while, he saw that Wu Li Chang had never moved from his spot in the living room. He did not appear surprised or shocked at what was happening in his apartment. He stood there patiently watching, as if waiting for it to be over so he could return to his regular business.

Brian's vision was clouding. He was gasping for air. He flailed his arms behind him in a futile attempt to reach his weapon.

It was gone.

In a last ditch effort, he located the cell phone in his pocket. He pulled it out and wildly pointed it towards the living room. With his last remaining breath he hit a button and an audible <click> could be heard.

He, too, slumped to the floor in death.

The assailants checked Danny and Brian's bodies for any signs of life. There were none. They then looked towards Wu Li, who was still standing as still as a statue in his living room.

"Dispose of them," he said, curtly.

The assailants began dragging the dead bodies towards the doorway of Wu Li's apartment. Once they were gone, Wu Li tidied up some of the furniture and knick-knacks that had been dislodged during the scuffle. He was surprised that there wasn't more blood.

Vitaly would be pleased, he thought. Wu Li would regain his honor. He had eliminated the threat that was following him. He had eliminated the threat to the operation. He smiled at his good fortune.

He saw the phone that Brian had been clutching in his hand. It was now lying on the floor in the hallway. Wu Li walked over and picked it up, glancing at the view-screen.

To his horror, he realized that his efforts may have been all for naught. Now he didn't dare tell Vitaly about what had happened in his apartment that afternoon.

He looked at the screen of the phone again in disbelief.

The message read simply - "Photo sent."

CHAPTER 24

Alan and Wendy arrived at Symantec's Mountain View, California headquarters late in the morning. The cross country flight – their third in the last few days – was uneventful.

They pulled into the parking garage of the modern glass and steel facility at 350 Ellis Street and had made their way to the reception area.

"Did you get us an appointment?" asked Alan, holding the outer door for Wendy.

"Not this time," she said. "If there is any wrong-doing going on here, I didn't want anyone to get wise and fly the coop. I thought we'd let the surprise and shock that an FBI and NSA ID can bring work for us – for once."

"This should be interesting," said Alan, as they walked up to the reception kiosk. A fresh-faced secretary wearing a headset looked up from her computer monitor to greet them

"Good morning," she said, "- and welcome to Symantec World Headquarters. How can I help you today?"

"Good morning," said Wendy, immediately flashing her NSA badge. Alan took his cue and flashed his FBI one as well. "My name is Agent Wendy Tosca, from the NSA. I'd like to speak with someone about anti-virus software."

The receptionist tensed up a bit, but continued in a professional tone.

"Is there anything more you can tell me so I can find someone to help you?" she said, "- a specific department, perhaps?"

"Anyone who might be involved with coding or sending out updates – like for example – Norton Anti-Virus Suite?" said Alan, smiling. He was trying to put the young receptionist at ease. It was working.

The receptionist tapped a few keys on her keyboard.

"You could try one of the System Architects for Norton," she said, smiling back at Alan and ignoring Wendy. "They are on the sixth floor – there's a separate reception desk there. Shall I call them and let them know you'll be coming up?" she added.

"That won't be necessary," said Wendy, "- we'll make our own way."

"Elevators are at the end of the hall," said the receptionist, who handed over two visitor badges to Alan and Wendy and logged them into the register. "Turn left when you exit on the sixth floor. You can return these badges to me before you exit, please."

"Thank you so much," said Alan. Wendy just rolled her eyes.

They got into the elevator and Wendy punched the sixth floor button.

"Laying it on a little thick there in reception, don't you think?" said Wendy.

"You get more flies with honey," said Alan, smiling a little.

"You came off like a creepy old man – honey," added Wendy.

"Jealousy – plain and simple," said Alan, chuckling a little.

They exited the elevator on the sixth floor and made their way to the next reception desk. Alan's charms had apparently not been as potent as he thought. The receptionist here was well aware they were coming – having been alerted by the main receptionist from downstairs.

"Good morning," he said. The receptionist also eyed the visitor badges, making sure they were in plain view. "You'll want to speak with Mr. Hamilton – our lead Norton update engineer. He's in the last office at the end of the hall."

The receptionist pointed down the hall towards the end of the corridor, where a closed door was clearly visible.

"I'll call ahead and let him know you're coming," said the receptionist.

Both Alan and Wendy nodded and headed down the hallway. They stopped at the office door and politely knocked.

"Just a second," came the voice from inside. Alan and Wendy heard some papers rustling and file cabinets being shut. In a few seconds the door opened.

"Hello, agents" said Garrett Hamilton. "Please - come in." Garrett motioned towards the two chairs opposite his desk.

"Thank you," said Wendy, entering. She was closely followed by Alan, who nodded his head in acknowledgement. "I'm Agent Tosca, this is Agent Silverman."

"I'm Garrett Hamilton," said Garrett, moving towards his side of the desk, but not offering to shake hands. As he sat down, Wendy and Alan also did so as well. "What can I do for you?"

The conversation was polite, but it was clearly obvious that Garrett was distressed. No one had asked a single question as of yet, but Garrett's forehead was already beginning to shine from sweat. He was fidgety in his chair and he wouldn't make direct eye contact with either Alan or Wendy. The world's worst poker player could have read that something was wrong.

"Are you OK, Mr. Hamilton?" said Alan. "You seem nervous."

"Me?" said Garrett, laughing nervously. "Uhh – no, I'm fine." He swallowed hard and cleared his throat. "You needed help with something?"

"Yes," said Wendy. "We were wondering about anti-virus update packages. How they work – who has access to their content – how they are distributed. Any background information at this point would be tremendously helpful."

"What's this about?" said Garrett. He was pulling on his collar, which suddenly seemed incredibly tight. "I haven't done anything wrong."

Wendy and Alan looked at each other.

"No one said you had, Mr. Hamilton," added Alan. "We're just looking for some basic information –that's all. Are you sure everything is all right?"

"Yes – um, well – I think I ate something bad at breakfast," stuttered Garrett. Garrett eyes became wider, and he was becoming more and more agitated. "Uh, could we continue this conversation out on one of the observation balconies? I think I need some air."

"Sure," said Wendy. "Lead the way."

Garrett got up from behind his desk and almost collapsed. Alan was quick to catch him and steadied him, throwing on of Garrett's arms over his shoulder.

"Take it easy," said Alan. "Breathe – you've got to breathe."

Garrett took in some shaky, overemphasized breaths. He was shaking like a leaf.

"Do you have an infirmary or first-aid station in the building?" asked Wendy. She was now also on her feet and moving to assist Alan.

"No – no first aid," said Garrett. "I just need some air."

Alan and Wendy continued to prop up Garrett as they exited his office. He motioned his head down towards a hallway on their right.

"That way," he said, in a whisper.

They slowly walked together down the corridor and towards a set of glass doors. The doors led out onto a small patio which overlooked the campus. There were several comfortable outdoor seats and a table present, but Garrett motioned towards the outer ledge. Alan and Wendy helped him towards it, and he leaned into the hard outer wall and let the late morning breeze cool his face. His clothes were soaked from sweat. He took a few deeps breaths and seemed to calm down a bit.

Alan still had hold of Garrett to steady him, but Wendy had let go and backed away a few feet.

"Obviously," said Wendy, "- you have something to tell us."

Alan was staring at Garrett, who was still looking out over the ledge. He closed his eyes in anguish.

"I should have never done it," he said. Alan again looked at Wendy.

"Done what, Mr. Hamilton?" asked Wendy.

Alan dropped his head and began to sob. "I knew it," he blubbered. "I knew it."

"Mr. Hamilton," said Alan. "Why don't you talk to us? Maybe we can help?"

"It's too late," said Garrett, continuing to cry into his hands, "- t-t-too late."

Garrett suddenly stood up dead straight. A vicious exit wound exploded from his back and he began to fall backwards – his eyes still open in wide amazement.

The cracking sound of the rifle report came just seconds later.

CHAPTER 25

"Shooter, shooter!" screamed Wendy as she rolled to the floor and towards the far wall for cover. "Alan, get down!"

She pulled her side-arm as she rolled, bringing it to bear on her perimeter.

Alan was a little stunned by watching Garrett being shot right in front of him and was slower to respond.

A second shot whizzed over his head as he started his dive for the floor, the bullet shattering the glass door of the patio's entrance behind him. The second rifle report could be heard.

"To the west!" screamed Wendy, pulling on Garrett's body – trying to get him out of harm's way. A pool of blood was quickly forming on the ground under him and he was groaning in pain.

Alan now had his side-arm drwan, but there seemed to be no one to aim it at. He worked on helping Wendy pull Garrett's body closer to the outer wall.

Garret's breath was coming in ragged patches. The bullet had entered his upper chest, assuring that the wound would quickly be fatal. He weakly pulled Alan towards him and attempted to speak.

"Code….." whispered Garrett. Alan put his ear closer to Garrett, trying to hear.

"Code - - - rigged," whispered Garrett again. He swallowed hard.

"Yes?" said Alan. "The code – its rigged?"

Garrett weakly nodded.

"Find - - - -Viktor," Garrett said. He took another ragged breath and began choking up blood. "V-V-Viktor…….Lorsov."

"Viktor Lorsov?" said Alan

Garrett nodded, closed his eyes, and collapsed. He was dead.

Wendy was still scanning the perimeter, her weapon pointed outward and at the ready. All three of them were behind the safety of the outer wall of the building, still hunched down on the patio.

"I guess we're getting closer to finding out what's going on," said Alan. He was leaning on the wall, crouched down like a baseball catcher.

"You sure know how to show a girl a good time, I'll say that," said Wendy.

They waited on the patio for what seemed like forever, but in reality was actually only about ten minutes. From the outside, they could hear sirens racing towards their location, and onlookers were gazing out the windows of various floors above them, trying to see what was going on.

It took another hour to explain what had happened to the local authorities. After that, Alan and Wendy were back in Garrett's office, looking for anything that might be useful.

"Who's this Viktor Lorsov?" said Wendy.

"You tell me and we'll both know," Alan added back in. "At least we know that the code is rigged – rigged with what we have no idea."

"You keep looking," she said. "I'll be right back." She got up and left the office.

Alan was going to ask her where she was headed, but she was out of the office and down the hall before he could stop her. Alan found a small date book in a bottom drawer and was thumbing through it. It was blank, except for a single number - written in clear ink on one of the middle pages.

Twelve digits.

Alan had been around the cyber-crimes division long enough to know what that number looked like.

It was an offshore bank account number.

He tore the page out and stuffed it into his pocket. It would take a while to trace the origin, and he didn't have the time or the equipment at the moment.

Wendy came back in, looking concerned.

"What's up?" asked Alan.

"More problems," said Wendy. "I just talked to another engineer. He said they just sent out a Norton update two days ago."

"That means that if the code was rigged, it's already been distributed," said Alan.

"Right," said Wendy, "- and I have more bad news."

She handed her phone over to Alan.

"We just got this picture sent over from the Hong Kong office," said Wendy.

Alan looked at the picture that was now on Wendy's phone. It showed a Chinese man standing in a living room of an apartment. Two men were lying in a blurry pile just in the foreground. The man in the background was not making any attempts to move. He was just staring at the scene that was taking place right in front of him.

"Who's this?" said Alan, scanning the photo.

"Well," said Wendy. "One of the blurry men on the floor is one of the CIA's field agents. He and another agent had been sent to pick up the Chinese man standing in the background."

Alan looked concerned. He knew there was more bad news coming.

"One of those agent's bodies was just pulled from the harbor in Kowloon Bay," said Wendy.

"That can't be good," said Alan. " - so who's the Chinese guy?"

"You're gonna love it," said Wendy. "That - - is Wu Li Chang."

Alan looked confused.

"He's our Chinese key-card holder."

CHAPTER 26

Alan and Wendy were seated in a secure conference room of the Los Angeles FBI field office. It had taken them almost ten minutes to convince Frank Alvis, their Pittsburgh hacker, that the line was not being tapped and that no one was recording their conversation. He was still being painfully evasive.

"For the last time Frank, no one is listening to this call but us," pleaded Wendy. "I don't know how else to convince you."

There was still silence on the other end of the line.

"Frank, this is Alan," added Alan. "We really need your help here."

Another few seconds of silence, then a voice came through the speaker phone.

"OK," said Frank. "This goes against my better judgment, but I'm going to trust you."

Both Alan and Wendy gave each other a look of relief.

"Thanks, Frank," said Wendy, "- we really need 'Tron007' on this one." She figured it couldn't hurt to boost Frank's ego a bit.

"Frank," said Alan, "- you were right about the Norton code. We met up with a system architect here and he confirmed that something malicious has been inserted into it."

"Well," said Frank,"- that should be easy then – just tell him to take it out."

Both Wendy and Alan looked at each other again, trying to decide who would break the news to Frank.

"That's the problem," said Wendy. "The code updates shipped two days ago."

There was a short pause on the other end of the line.

"That is a problem," said Frank. "Norton distributes worldwide, so I'm sure it's been pushed everywhere by now. Do you know what the bug is?"

"No," said Alan, "- but we're assuming it's like you explained to us earlier – something to either mask or destroy the DNS resolution database table."

"Does the system architect know what it is?" said Frank. "He should be able to identify the specific code. Any updates have to get their buy-off before the package is zipped up and shipped out. Even so, if the "Sys-Arch" knows what it is, they can package up a fix to neutralize it and re-ship an emergency update. "

"That's one of our other problems," said Wendy. "The "Sys-Arch" is dead."

"Dead?" said Frank, sounding both shocked and worried at the same time. "That's a BIG problem. Have they informed the end-user community?"

"We talked to their execs," said Alan. "They basically threw us out of the room. All we could tell them was that we had reason to believe that there was bad code that was sent out. We have no proof."

"Plus, the Symantec Board of Directors didn't want to cause a panic," said Wendy.

"Which would kill their reputation and stock price," added Frank. "That's an awfully big risk they are taking. If this code really does execute what I think it does – it could be "lights out" all over whenever the bug is triggered."

"Is there anything else you can do?" asked Alan.

Frank thought for a moment. The phone was silent.

"Give me some time," said Frank. "I might be able to hack into a corporate system that has downloaded the update. If I can take a look at the code, maybe I can tell you what's wrong with it – and where it came from."

"That's a start," said Frank. "How do you plan on doing that?"

"I'd rather not say - quite frankly," added Frank.

"Fair enough," added Alan.

"How much time do you need?" asked Wendy.

"Give me four hours," said Frank.

"You've got two," added Wendy. "We'll be in touch." She hung up the phone.

"Why the pressure?" asked Alan. "I'd think you'd want to give this guy all the time he needs."

"We don't have the time," she added. "We'll be on the move again – very soon."

"Great," said Alan, faking his enthusiasm – poorly. "I sure hope it's another plane ride."

"Your wish is my command," said Wendy, smiling. "You have a passport on file?" she asked.

"Uhh, yeah – why?" he replied, looking at her warily.

"Our friend 'Tron007' told us the fake system messages looked Chinese," said Wendy, laying out her case. "The picture that was sent to us was of Wu Li Chang, our Chinese key-holder. The CIA agents who were sent to pick him up are found in Kowloon Harbor. Look at Wu Li in that picture. He doesn't seem concerned at all that there is a death struggle going on right in front of him. Something doesn't add up. You don't believe in coincidence on this job, do you?"

"Nope," said Alan. He knew exactly where they were headed.

"Then pack a bag, partner," she added. "We're going to Hong Kong."

CHAPTER 27

Wu Li Chang was back in Vitaly Lukashenko's office that overlooked the Hong Kong Operations Center.

Vitaly was sipping on a drink, gently swirling the ice and vodka around in an expensive crystal tumbler. He was facing the monitors in his large swivel chair, monitoring the news reports. More unrest in the Ukraine. This time the Russians had sent a fleet of trucks across the border, masquerading as humanitarian aid to the region. It was a flimsy cover story, and even the anchors delivering the news didn't believe it. It was clear this was more weapons and ammunition to support the unrest.

The West had hastily approved harsher economic sanctions in response to the Russian actions, but it did not seem to deter their activity.

Vitaly clenched his teeth. The images were disturbing. Homes and farms were being burned to the ground, livestock was being slaughtered – innocent people were hoarding all of their belongings into cars and wagons, trying to flee the area. Where would they go? Vitaly knew that there was nowhere to go – and that the Russians would be merciless to the locals if they remained in the region.

Wu Li cleared his throat slightly to announce his presence.

"Yes?" came the reply from the chair back.

"Our Symantec system architect has been eliminated, per our operational plan," reported Wu Li. He didn't dare report that the strike team had missed the chance to eliminate both of the American agents. There would be time to correct that mistake.

"Good," said Vitaly. "Cancel the wire transfer of our payment to Mr. Hamilton."

"Already done," added Wu Li.

"What's our collection status on the key-cards?" asked Vitaly. He knew very well what the status was, but he wanted to hear it again.

"We currently have four out of the seven key-cards in our possession," recited Wu Li. "Two are in the hands of the Americans – the last key in Burkina Faso has yet to be located, but you ordered that extraction cancelled."

"Four out of seven is fine," said Vitaly, "- ICANN can no longer stop our plans. Keep me informed of any other updates."

The tone of Vitaly's voice meant that Wu Li was being summarily dismissed. He turned to leave.

"One more thing," said Vitaly.

Wu Li stopped short. "Yes?"

"The American agents," came the voice from behind the chair, "- have they been dealt with?"

Wu Li winced. It was not a subject he wanted to bring up.

"We're still working on an available opportunity to deal with that problem," Wu Li lied.

"Get it done, Wu," ordered Vitaly. "I don't want them sharing what they know with anyone else. This operation will move forward as scheduled."

"As you wish," added Wu Li, bowing. He turned and quickly left.

Vitaly returned his concentration and gaze to the monitors as he took a small sip of his drink. He would deal with the Russians in his own way.   He would also ensure that the rest of the world was reminded as to what happens when they let innocents suffer and do nothing.

Soon.

Very soon.

CHAPTER 28

Wendy and Alan sat in a small conference room attached to the American Airlines Sky Lounge at San Francisco International Airport. They were waiting to catch the non-stop flight from San Francisco to Hong Kong, which was going to be leaving within the hour. They had one last phone call to make before they got into the air for their almost fifteen-hour flight westward.

"Frank, this is Wendy- you've had two hours, what have you got?" she said into the conference room's speaker phone.

"Wow," said Frank, "- you people are tough."

"I know you have something for me," she added. She could almost see 'Tron007' smiling in his apartment, almost three-thousand miles away.

"I do," said Frank, "- but you're not going to like it."

"I'll hold her up, Frank," said Alan. "Give us the bad news."

"Well," said Frank, "- from a coding point of view, its actually pretty sweet. I accessed the files on the 'Home Depot' system. The code itself remains dormant as one of twenty-eight updates being pushed with the latest Norton Anti-Virus Suite update."

"What do you mean — 'dormant'?" asked Alan.

"That means," continued Frank, "- that is loads itself onto the target system, but doesn't do anything until it's activated by a remote user. That's usually done by issuing a command from some master system."

"But if the code is already on the systems," said Wendy, "- can't you just take it off?"

"That's the beauty of this design," said Frank. "The code that's there is innocent, but once the activation key is received it unpacks more hidden code onto the host system and begins executing it."

"So it's a hidden time bomb, just waiting for someone to set it off," said Alan.

"Exactly," said Frank. "Now that it's on there, it can stay there for hours, days, even weeks before its activated, but once it happens — they'll be nothing to stop it."

"Can't we devise a patch or hot-fix and upload that to all of the infected systems?" asked Wendy.

"Patch or fix what?" said Frank. "That's the big problem here - we don't know what the virus will do or how it works. We have to know the disease before we can devise a cure."

"And by that time it may be too late," said Alan.

"Not necessarily," said Frank.

"You mean you can fix it?" said Alan in surprise. He was looking over at Wendy, hoping they wouldn't have to get onboard the long overseas flight after all.

"Eventually – yes," said Frank. "Once I see what the code is doing, I can devise a patch for it."

"But that means we have to unleash the beast before it can be slayed," said Wendy.

"Yes," said Frank.

Wendy looked over at Frank and shook her head, indicating that the flight was still on. Alan winced.

"Isn't there anything you can do?" said Alan.

"Possibly," said Frank. "The execution command will have to originate from some starting point. It will fan out across the network in all directions, activating the virus as it goes. Think of the ripples in the water when you toss a rock into a pond."

"How does that help?" asked Wendy.

"If I can see what systems are being infected," said Frank, "- I can try to get out ahead of the spread and kill the network links that allow it to propagate. That should stop any other systems from receiving the execution command and contain the impact."

"That sounds awfully tricky," said Alan. "Are you sure you can do that?"

"As long as I can narrow down where to look, I'll have a much better chance of catching it at the start," said Frank. "If I can witness the initial impact ring — say within five minutes of its first effects — I'd say I have a '50-50' chance to get out in front of it."

Wendy and Alan looked at each other.

"Those aren't the best odds," Alan said.

"Better than most," said Frank. "Besides, I think we're on the right track as to the malicious code's point of origin. I'm still confident it's Chinese."

"I hope you're right," said Wendy. "We're about to jump on a plane for Hong Kong. There's a man we have to find there."

"Can you monitor any Chinese systems?" said Alan. "Specifically, can you watch Hong Kong for any weird activity?"

"'Tron007' can do almost anything," said Frank.

"It's a risk," said Wendy, "- but right now it's all we've got. We're either going to be right - - "

"Or very, very wrong," said Alan, interrupting.

"I'll drop some monitors and sniffers in on some network routes in and out of Hong Kong," said Frank, "- and see if I can come up with anything."

"Good man," said Wendy. "We'll call you if we need you, but it will be a while before we land."

"I'm tracking your flight already," said Frank.

"How the...?" said Alan.

Wendy just smiled and hung up the phone.

"Remind me to change some of my account passwords," said Alan.

"Come on," Wendy said, smiling. "We have a plane to catch."

They left the American Airlines Sky Lounge and made their way to the gate. As they passed their tickets off to the attendant and headed down the boarding ramp, a stranger standing in the terminal pulled out his cell phone and dialed in an overseas number.

"Yes?" came the curt response on the far end. It was Wu Li Chang who answered.

"Targets have just boarded a non-stop flight for Hong Kong – American Airlines," said the stranger. "They should be arriving in about fifteen hours."

"Thank you," said Wu Li. He quickly hung up the phone.

So the Americans were coming to him? All the better.
He'd take care of this problem, once and for all.

CHAPTER 29

Alan was completely wiped out. Even though they had been booked in business class for the trans-Pacific flight and had long seats that converted into makeshift beds, he had hardly slept at all. He spent most of the flight mindlessly watching the in-flight entertainment offerings, even sitting through three complete viewings of 'The Avengers' movie. By the time they landed in Hong Kong, he was unshaven, groggy, and irritable.

Wendy was just the opposite. She was used to field work – along with the long slogs of boring travel that often accompanied it - and had fallen asleep soon after take-off. She was looking fresh and energetic as they both left the airport and walked up to the taxi stand. Wendy confidently addressed the attendant.

"*Qing jiao chu zu che,*" said Wendy - in excellent Mandarin.

Alan just stared at her. "You're not serious," he said.

"Oh yeah," she grinned at him, "- took it at the Academy. I'm a little rusty, but we'll get by."

A cab was quickly called for the pretty American lady who knew Mandarin and her shabby friend. They piled into the cab, and Wendy gave the driver the address.

"Please tell me we're headed to a hotel," said Alan.

"Nope," said Wendy. "We need to go check out our Chinese key-card holder's address. See if there's anything the locals missed. Buck up, sailor – we're not taking any naps yet."

"Fantastic," said Alan. He stared out the window. This was his first time in Hong Kong, but he was too tired to enjoy it. It was such a mix of old and new - of history and technology. Modern, gleaming towers reached up to the skies, while antique paddle boats and junks plied the waters of Kowloon Bay. Alan didn't seem to care. He shut his eyes for the few minutes of rest he could steal on the cab ride.

Further back, keeping a safe distance – two motorcycles deftly followed the cab. One would turn off every few blocks leaving a solo rider – only to return a few streets later, so as to not draw suspicion. Alan was certainly not looking, and Wendy was enjoying the views that Hong Kong had to offer.

After a ride of about twenty minutes, they turned into a mixed use area of the city. It contained apartment towers with several first-floor shops and markets.

It was late in the evening and the sun had already set behind the Hong Kong skyline. Various neon lights from signs and other businesses were beginning to flicker on, and the streets took on the look of a garish international carnival.

Wendy spoke a few words to the cab driver, who pulled over to the curb along a residential street.

"Wake up, cowboy," said Wendy, nudging Alan.

"Damn it, woman," said Alan, "- I hear you." He rubbed his eyes and took a long pull on his face, shaking his head to become fully awake.

Wendy was already out of the taxi door. The cool evening air hit Alan head on. He was overtaken by all of the strange smells of the city. They were totally foreign to him. He joined Wendy on the sidewalk and she started off down the street.

"What about our bags?" said Alan. Even though they had only each brought a small carry-on, Alan was still concerned.

"I told him to wait," said Wendy. "C'mon, this won't take long. Then we can go back to the hotel and you can get some sleep."

At the far end of the street, one motorcycle and its mysterious rider had taken up position. The other rider was currently nowhere in sight. A large panel van was also parked three spaces away from the entrance of Wu Li's apartment building.

Wendy had started across the street. She was already over and getting ready to make her way up the small steps to Wu Li's building as Alan - who was lagging behind was just starting across the street behind her.

She heard the van door open and instinctively reacted.

In one motion, Wendy had pulled her side-arm and had tucked herself into a barrel-roll, aiming her body for a large planter beside the entrance of the building.

Three armed men had exited the van. One was already crouched and taking his first shot at Wendy. The bullet whizzed over her head as she had tucked into her roll. The second man was taking up a support position behind the parked vehicle behind the van and was also facing in Wendy's direction.

"Alan!" shouted Wendy. "Get down!"

Alan was shaken to his senses by Wendy's warning and had immediately ducked and headed for the cover of the parked car directly in front of him.

The third man from the van had come between the cars and was now standing in the street, lowering his weapon on Alan. Alan pulled his side-arm and spun to face his attacker, who now had him dead in his sights.

A shot rang out from the doorway of the apartment building. It ripped through the shoulder of the third attacker, who fell sideways out into the street from the concussion. His weapon fell from his hands and bounced in the street - going off - but spraying the bullet uselessly in the opposite direction.

Alan glanced over at Wendy's position. She had re-aimed at her own attackers and was laying down return fire towards the van. Incoming shots were slamming into the side of the building, spraying concrete and debris all over the street.

Alan changed his angle and was now also firing towards the remaining two assailants from the van. The few people that were out and about in the streets had all taken cover, some screaming as they ran away.

Wendy emptied her first clip and was reloading a second. The two assailants had better position on her and she was pinned down. Alan was trying to make his way closer to the two attackers, slowly inching his way along his cover car on the street side.

The mystery rider of the motorcycle at the far end of the street was watching the whole scene unfold. His job was simply to report their position to the extraction team and offer any aid, if needed. From his vantage point, the extraction team had the upper hand thus far, even if they had already lost one team member.

Wendy was still pinned down and couldn't see Alan on the far side of the parked cars. Where was he? It seemed like an eternity since he had fired his weapon. Was he hit?

The answer to her question came quickly, as Alan rose up and unleashed a furious barrage of cover fire from the parked vehicle. The two assailants hunkered down and Wendy took the opportunity to get out from behind the planter and retreat back into the lobby of the apartment building. The windows had been shattered in the opening exchange - the crunching of glass could be easily heard underneath Wendy's shoes as she fell back into a better covered position.

The firing had ceased from Alan's position. He was obviously out of ammo and was reloading, crouched back down along the car on the street side. The two assailants had also taken a break and were determining their next move.

Wendy heard the roar of the motorcycle engine from her new position in the apartment building lobby.

The second motorcycle was quickly coming up the street and bearing down on their location. She looked out towards where Alan was hidden and could just see the top of Alan's head through the parked car window. His back was facing the oncoming motorcycle.

"Alan – behind you!" she shouted.

She couldn't be heard from the noise of the revving motorcycle engine, which had now reached a high speed and was hurtling towards Alan on the street in front of her. The driver of the second motorcycle lowered his head and braced for the impact.

"Look out!" she shouted again, wide eyed.

It was too late. There was a horrible thud, and Alan Silverman was airborne, his weapon leaving his hand.

CHAPTER 30

It was like something out of a Hollywood action movie. From Wendy's vantage point, she saw Alan flying through the air, followed by the motorbike that had just crashed into him. The whole scene was playing itself out in slow motion.

The second motorcycle rider had flipped completely over his handlebars and was also airborne. The motorcycle had taken a turn into the parked car where Alan had previously been crouched down, when he was trying to stay out of the way of the two attackers from the van. The bike's front end was crumpling into the rear passenger door of the car, inertia whipping the back of the bike around and into the front passenger door.

The motorcyclist was anticipating the impact, and had balled up his body, lowering his head and rolling over as he slammed back into the pavement. He continued to roll over and over, allowing the friction of the street to slow him down, his padded suit taking the blows of the roadway.

Alan; however, had not expected the crash. His limbs were flying seemingly in all directions as he was airborne. He was wide eyed and surprised. He slammed into the pavement and actually bounced – not once, but twice. He rolled and rolled – coming to a stop as a lifeless lump lying in the street and unconscious.

Time regained its proper speed for Wendy.

"Noooooooo!" she shouted, and emerged from her position, taking up a triangular stance and renewing her fire towards the two attackers who were crouched down behind the van.

At this point the first motorcycle rider at the far end of the street started his bike and raced towards the scene.

The second cyclist was now on his feet – a bit shaky, but he had already grabbed Alan and was pulling him towards the van.

Wendy saw what was happening. They were attempting to abduct Alan, and she was having none of it. She switched her position and began firing at the second motorcyclist. Her first shot caught him under the left side of his chest. He slumped forward and dropped Alan, a mere two feet from the van's side door.

The two attackers were now renewing their barrage on Wendy. She was forced to fall back again into the lobby of the building.

The first cyclist had now reached Alan. He dropped his bike and slid open the van door, hauling Alan inside. He then jumped into the driver's seat and started the van, which was the signal for the other two attackers that it was time to leave.

Wendy checked her weapon - she only had two shots remaining.

The first attacker fell back and jumped in the open side door of the van. The van had now pulled out and was getting ready to exit. The second attacker took one last look at the lobby and dropped back – he also entered the van through its open side door. He slammed the door shut as the van accelerated hard, starting up the street.

Wendy rolled out and took her two final shots, taking out one tail light on the van. The van turned the corner at the end of the street and disappeared.

Wendy found herself breathing hard, the adrenaline really kicking in now that it was all over. She was shaking in the street, which was littered with concrete debris, shattered glass, and two abandoned motorcycles – once a twisted heap and the other lying prone in the middle of the roadway.

In a last ditch effort, she ran over to the functional motorcycle, but there were no keys left behind to start it.

The whole block was now strangely quiet. People were still hidden - not sure if it was all over. In the distance, Wendy could hear incoming sirens.

Alan was gone, and she had to move.

Surprisingly, her cab driver had done his duty and not left the area. Actually, he had been too scared to move at all. Wendy jumped in the cab and ordered him to get moving. In the shock of the moment, he quietly obeyed and they sped off.

CHAPTER 31

Alan lay in the back of the van - groggy, sore, and disoriented. It seemed like every part of his body was hurting. He didn't remember much about the accident. All he knew was his back was to the street, he thought he heard shouting – then the high pitched whine of a motorcycle engine. Suddenly, he remembered, he was off of his feet, flying through the air – and now he was in the back of a van.

Every now and then he heard voices. A few words of Chinese, delivered in quick, clipped tones. It was dark outside. Flashes of neon occasionally penetrated the front windows, casting a colorful hue to the occupants up front. One person was crouched in the back of the empty van. Every so often he would turn to look at Alan, making sure he had stayed put.

No worry in that, thought Alan. It hurt too much to move all together.

After a few more turns, the light coming inside the front of the van changed. It was now steadily white – and he could feel the van descending and turning.

A parking garage – it had to be.

The van soon came to a stop, and two of the occupants piled into the back to retrieve Alan. The driver opened the side door of the van, allowing light to pour into the back. Alan turned his head and closed his eyes from the sudden brightness, and he groaned as he was dragged out of the van and stood up on his feet outside of the van.

Another Chinese man was standing in front of him now.

"Can you walk?" asked the stranger.

Alan was confused. The man was speaking English.

"I said - can you walk?" came the question again.

Alan now opened his eyes and focused in on who was speaking to him.

It was Wu Li Chang, the holder of the Chinese key-card.

"I – uhhhh – yes - - - -I think so," said Alan, still groggy.

"Good," said Wu Li. He then barked a few orders in Chinese at the other men. The two who had retrieved him out of the back of the van escorted him across the parking garage – Wu Li leading the way. It was slow going for Alan, who staggered and stumbled at first before regaining his balance and footing. One of the escorts was quick to push Alan on the shoulder when he was not making adequate progress.

They stopped in front of an elevator. Wu Li pushed a button on the doorway and the doors slid open. The entire party entered and turned to face the doors as they closed. The elevator began moving up.

"Where are we?" asked Alan.

"Be quiet!" said Wu Li. "You will speak only when spoken to – is that clear?"

Alan was taken aback a bit by the ferocity of Wu Li's tone. He nodded his head that he understood.

After a short ride, the elevator doors opened and the party stepped out into the foyer.

They had emerged into a state-of-the-art data center. Sleek consoles were spread out around the room, each manned by a busy operator equipped with a headset. The consoles were all facing towards Wu Li and his emerging party. A glow of light was casting from above and behind them, and Alan craned his neck around to see a large wall of monitors and video screens each showing different charts, data, and maps of the world and specific geographic regions. The room itself was darkly lit, the bulk of the light emanating from individual operator consoles and the large wall of video screens on the wall behind Alan.

On the far side of the room, Alan could see metal steps that rose up to an elevated platform. On this platform was a glass enclosed room. Alan could see several small monitors all over the far wall. He could also see the rear of a high-backed swivel chair, which was turned away from the room.

One of Alan's captor's pushed him again, and motioned for him to follow Wu Li, who was making his way across the Operations floor and towards the metal staircase that led to the elevated office. He followed, making his way as best he could.

It took him a few extra seconds to slowly navigate the stairs, but soon they were all outside the glass enclosed office.

Wu Li turned and said something to the two escorts, who bowed and took one step back.

"Come with me," said Wu Li. He opened the door to the office. Alan followed him in.

They took up a position on the opposite side of a large desk that was in the center of the room, their backs now facing the Operations floor. The chair in front of them had not turned around, but Alan knew it was occupied, because a long trail of cigarette smoke could be seen slowly circling up from behind it. The monitors showed various news feeds from around the world. On one he could clearly see tanks and heavy equipment moving on roads – the caption looked Russian.

Wu Li cleared his throat.

"Yes?" said Vitaly.

"I've brought you a visitor," he said.

The chair slowly swiveled around. Alan could now see its occupant. A tall, well- built man wearing what looked like a dark and expensive - looking turtleneck sweater. He had long blonde hair which was pulled back in a neat ponytail. His eyes were a strange gray color, and they were carefully studying Alan from across the desk. He did not speak for a few moments, but then spoke to Wu Li.

"And who is this?" asked Vitaly. Alan could hear the distinct tinge of a Russian accent in the man's voice.

"This is one of the American agents who has been causing us so much trouble," said Wu Li.

There was a slight pause. Vitaly took another long pull from his cigarette, the smoke exiting lazily from his nostrils and mouth.

"I thought my instructions were very clear," said Vitaly, "- you were told to eliminate the American agents, not bring them here.

"That's the problem," said Wu Li. "They are in Hong Kong. I thought – "

"Your opinion in this matter is of no concern to me, Wu," interrupted Vitaly.

Wu paused for a moment, embarrassed that he had been dishonored yet again – and this time in front of a lowly prisoner.

"I thought," continued Wu, "- that it might be useful to find out what this man knows before we get rid of him. I thought it was the right thing to do."

Vitaly looked Alan up and down again, sizing him up and making a decision.

"This man knows nothing," stated Vitaly, dismissing Alan almost at once. "Take him somewhere and get rid of him – and his partner as well."

Alan quickly jumped into the conversation. He felt he had to say something, if only to delay his own execution.

"She knows what I know," said Alan. Wu Li looked surprised. It was unheard of to speak in Vitaly's presence without first being asked a direct question.

Vitaly took another drag of his cigarette. "You don't know anything," said Vitaly.

"I know that Wu Li Chang here is a key-card holder for the DNSSEC reboot sequence," said Alan, pointing at Wu Li.

"Common knowledge," said Vitaly. "Anyone with an internet connection could find out that information."

"I know that you are behind all of the recent DNS outages, and that you've rigged the recent Norton Anti-Virus updates with malicious code," said Alan.

Vitaly stared at Alan. It was a good game of chicken. Alan could be guessing, but he had peaked Viatly's interest.

Alan could see that he had an opening.

"And we know that you're behind the disappearance – and I'm going to assume, killings, of three of the other key-card holders," said Alan.

"And why would I need to do that?" asked Vitaly.

"To keep ICANN from resetting the system," said Alan. "We've already reported this in to headquarters. They are tracking my partner and me right now. This place will soon be crawling with agents."

Alan had pushed the conversation too far with his last statement. It was a lie. He knew it.

And so did Vitaly.

Still, he didn't like loose ends. He decided he wanted Alan's partner taken into custody as well. The operation was going to be executed very soon, and he didn't need any possible unforeseen circumstance to delay it. He knew that once "Apokalypsis" was initiated, nothing either of the agents or their government knew could stop it.

Wu Li jumped into the conversation.

"I can bring the girl in," he stated, confidently.

"I don't think that will be necessary," said Vitaly. "As a matter of fact, I think she'll come to us."

Both Alan and Wu Li were puzzled by the last statement.

"Take this man and hold him in one of the offices – for now," said Vitaly.

"As you wish," said Wu Li, bowing. He grabbed Alan by the arm and pulled him out of the office to the escort detail outside on the raised platform.

Vitaly swiveled his chair back around and faced the video monitors in his office.

If the U.S. government really did know about him, the Operations Center would already be raided by now, Vitaly thought. Americans – they always rush in, never playing any long term strategy. Always force, force, force – just like the Russians. No finesse.

The battered agent they had captured would be useful for a while longer.

CHAPTER 32

The Renaissance Harbour View Hotel in downtown Hong Kong offers spectacular views of Victoria Harbor. Sadly, Wendy Tosca was not interested in the view – at least not tonight.

She was blankly looking out over the Hong Kong cityscape, having been dropped off by the cab driver who had been frightened out of his wits by the earlier events of the evening. He had witnessed a shoot-out, a kidnapping, a horrible accident, and a killing. The quicker he had unloaded his passenger, the better.

Wendy had brought both carry-ons into her room. She checked her weapon, which had experienced more use tonight than at any time in her NSA career. Wendy had gone through three clips and was now completely out of ammunition. She had lost her friend and partner to what was clearly some sort of hit team that had been tipped off to their arrival.

Now that the excitement had dwindled down, she too felt the aches and pains of muscles that had been called upon for rapid action. She needed a drink – and a long, hot shower.

She pulled a Jack Daniels from the mini-bar and uncapped it, downing the entire miniature bottle in one smooth gulp. The alcohol burned on the way down, but tasted so, so good.

She stood under the hot shower for a good twenty-five minutes, letting the water soak over her bumps and bruises. It also had given her time to think.

They were obviously on the right track coming to Hong Kong. Their hacker contact, Frank Alvis, had apparently correctly predicted the code's origin, and there was the strange motivation of Wu Li Chang, the Chinese DNSSEC reboot key- card holder. Why didn't he want to be picked up? Was he involved in all of this somehow?

Then there was Alan. She didn't know if he was dead or alive. He had taken a ferocious hit from that speeding motorbike and had been pulled – either unconscious or dead – into the white panel van and removed from the street where Wu Li's apartment was located.

Wendy was in a bit of a predicament. She was facing something she hadn't had to deal with in all of her years of service – from her time at the Naval Academy through her field experience at the NSA.

She didn't know what to do next.

She stepped out of the shower, put on one of the plush hotel robes, and wrapped her head in a spare towel. She came back into the room, grabbed another Jack Daniels from the mini-bar, and this time poured it into a glass with some ice.

She plopped down into a chair, leaned back and closed her eyes, letting out a massive sigh. The stress of the flight (even though she had slept) and the evening's events quickly overtook her and she had drifted off into a light sleep.

She was jarred awake by the ringing of her room phone.

She picked up the receiver.

"*Ni hao?*" she said, uttering her greeting in Chinese.

"You speak Chinese, Ms. Tosca?" said a voice on the other end. It had a distinct Russian accent.

"Who is this?" said Wendy, quickly switching back to English and straightening up in her chair.

"The man you and your partner have been looking for," said Vitaly.

"You killed him," said Wendy, the anger rising in her voice.

"Come, come, Ms. Tosca," said Vitaly. "You partner is alive – and in reasonable health – for now."

Wendy was relieved to hear that Alan was still among the living.

"What do you want?" said Wendy.

"Oh, it's not what I want," said Vitaly, " – it's what YOU want."

"And that is?" said Wendy.

"You want to keep your partner alive," said Vitaly. "I need to speak to you."

"So speak," said Wendy.

There was a chuckle from the end of the line.

"We both know that what we have to talk about can't be discussed over the phone," said Vitaly.

Wendy was silent for a moment.

"What do you propose?" she said.

"Get some sleep, Ms. Tosca," said Vitaly. "I'm sure you've earned it after the long flight and your exciting evening. I will send a car by tomorrow to pick you up at say – 09:00?"

Wendy was hesitant. If the stranger on the phone knew who she was and where she was, there was nothing to stop another party from attacking her yet tonight – and she was out of ammunition.

"Ms. Tosca, you have my word as a gentleman," said Vitaly. "If I had wanted you dead – you'd be dead. Get some rest – we will speak in the morning."

"I guess I don't have much of a choice," Wendy added.

"That is correct," said Vitaly, "- until tomorrow then?"

"Until tomorrow," said Wendy. The line went dead.

At least she knew Alan was alive. That was good news. Who was the mystery man? The man with the Russian accent? He obviously wielded power, and was probably the architect of this whole scheme.

She took a long gulp of the Jack Daniels, again draining the glass.

Tomorrow would bring answers – whether she liked them or not.

CHAPTER 33

Wendy Tosca did not have a good night's sleep.

Every creak or echo from either the hotel room or out in the hallway had her on edge. She felt sure that an attempt would be made to apprehend her during the night, but in this case, Vitaly Lukashenko had been true to his word.

Wendy finally got out of bed after fitful bouts of on-and-off light napping, took another shower to freshen up, and headed down to the hotel lobby.

She was slowly making her way towards the door, when she was approached by two Oriental men in suit coats.

"Ms. Tosca?" said the first, very politely.

"Yes," replied Wendy.

"Before we depart, I must first ask for your cell phone and weapon, if you please," said the first man, this time extending his hand.

Wendy's weapon was useless, as she had no more ammunition. She quietly handed it over. She then took out her cell phone and handed it to the second man, who extended his hand to take it. He took the phone and made sure it was off, then slipped it into his pocket.

"Right this way, if you please," said the first man, directing her to follow him. The second man fell in behind Wendy and they calmly exited the building. Outside, a car was waiting, a driver already behind the wheel. The first man opened the back door of the sedan for Wendy and motioned for her to enter. The second man went around the car and entered the back seat from the far side. The first man then followed Wendy into the back seat, sandwiching her in between both men.

The sedan was roomy, so the back seat did not feel cramped.

The first man removed a small blindfold from the seatback, similar to a sleeping mask.

"Ms. Tosca," said the first man, "- if you'll put this on, please." He handed the mask to Wendy, who put it on. The first man then waved his had in front of Wendy to ensure she could not see. Satisfied that her vision was obstructed, he then nodded his head to the driver, who was watching for the signal via the rear view mirror. Once received, he smoothly pulled out into traffic.

The ride took about ten minutes, and Wendy, too, recognized the darkened surroundings and multiple turns as signs they were entering a parking garage.

The car came to a stop.

"You may remove your blindfold now," said the first man.

Wendy took off the sleep mask and tried to regain her bearings. They were definitely in some sort of underground parking structure, but there were no distinguishing marks or signs to indicate what building they were in.

Wendy was led to a nearby elevator. She and the two escorts entered the lift, the second man punched in a number, and they were whisked upwards to the data center's Operations floor.

As they exited the elevator, Wu Li Chang was waiting for them.

"Good morning, Ms. Tosca," said Wu Li. "Right this way, please."

He motioned for her to follow him. They walked through the Operations floor area and ascended a set of steps to a glass enclosed office that overlooked the data center. A large swivel chair was turned away from them towards a bank of monitors on the far side of the office wall. Through the windows, she could see Alan sitting in a chair that had been placed on the near side of a large desk.

Alan was still battered and bruised, but he had slept, been fed, and was allowed to shave and clean himself up, so he looked better than he had when he arrived. His eyes met Wendy's as they entered the glass office.

She smiled at Alan, showing a look of relief that he was alive. He returned the smile with a weak grin of his own and gave her a look that indicated that he was OK.

"Good to see you," she said.

"Silence," snapped Wu Li. "You will speak only when spoken to."

"Now, Now, Wu," said a voice from behind the chair. "That's no way to treat our guests."

Wu Li bowed his head to the high backed chair and took a step backward. "As you wish," he simply said.

Wendy recognized the voice immediately as the man who had called her at the hotel the night before.

"I trust you slept well, Ms. Tosca?" said the chair back.

"Not really," said Wendy, "- but you kept your word."

"Oh, I always keep my promises," said the chair. He slowly swiveled around to face Wendy, Alan, and Wu Li from across the mammoth desk. Wendy took note of the tall man with long blonde hair pulled back into a neat ponytail. He had on a tailored suit and a perfectly matched tie in a neat Windsor knot. His whole demeanor spoke to the fact that he was certainly the man in charge.

"I believe it's time for some formal introductions," said Vitaly.

"My name is Vitaly Lukashenko," he said. "Welcome to my data facility. From here you will soon witness the collapse of Western Civilization as you both know it."

CHAPTER 34

Vitaly waved Wu Li out of the room. Wu Li bowed again - then exited, leaving Vitaly alone with Alan and Wendy.

Vitaly stared at both of them across his desk for a few minutes. Alan and Wendy both looked at each other, shocked by what Vitaly had just told them. He patiently lit up a cigarette.

"You must have questions," said Vitaly, "- now is the time to ask them."

Alan glanced over at Wendy again. He figured he'd start.

"Vitaly Lukashenko?" said Alan. "Didn't you run the Russian company 'Utkonos' at one time?"

"I am impressed," said Vitaly. "Most Americans pay little attention to the rest of the world. I am surprised you even knew of its existence."

Alan looked at Wendy. "Mr. Lukashenko here founded the leading e-commerce site operating in Russia. He sold it off a few years ago – supposedly made a killing."

"I did well," added Vitaly.

"So why all of this?" said Wendy, waving her hand around the office and data center.

"Take a look at these monitors," said Vitaly, pointing behind him. "Are you familiar the Ukrainian crisis?"

They both nodded.

"We've seen the news," said Wendy.

"Yes," said Vitaly, " - yes - - -everyone has, and yet no one does anything about it."

"I thought the U.S. and Europe had applied economic sanctions," said Alan.

"Sanctions!" shouted Vitaly. Then he recomposed himself.

"Sanctions?" he continued, this time his voice under control. "Oh yes, the West has applied its 'sanctions'. You see the results of their failed efforts on the screens behind you. Take a good look at the people on those screens behind me. MY people. My home. It has been taken over – and yet the West stands and watches."

"The Ukrainians are fighting back," said Wendy.

"Oh yes, Ms. Tosca," said Vitaly, sarcastically. "They are fighting back – using antiquated technology and weapons. It's as if they have brought sticks to a knife fight. My people are no match for the Russian army – everyone realizes that, but to avoid escalating the confrontation, they capitulate. Study your history - the same thing happened with Germany in the late 1930's. The West stood by as Hitler annexed land and countries – and did nothing until it was too late."

"So how is what you're doing here going to help?" said Alan.

"I intend to create a level playing field," said Vitaly, "-economically speaking. The entire world will soon see what a real 'sanction' looks like."

"So why take it out on the world?" said Wendy. "Why not just punish the Russians."

"It's the hubris of the West that annoys me," said Vitaly. "The Americans are the worst. You think of yourselves as THE world power, but you are part of a declining civilization. You're more interested in reality television than the reality of life."

He was standing now, his voice rising and he was pacing behind his desk as he talked.

"You expect everything – instant gratification - but will give nothing in return," Vitaly continued. "You use your power for your own self-interests instead of helping the world. If my country sold you more oil, you'd have invaded with tanks and planes by now - as you did in Iraq and Afghanistan. There's nothing for you in the Ukraine, so that's what you offer as a solution – nothing. Europe is becoming more and more like YOU."

He pointed at both Alan and Wendy. He realized he was losing control of his temper. He took a deep breath and sat down.

"The Russians," said Vitaly, "- are only part of the problem. To get people to listen, you first have to get their attention."

"So crushing the internet is your way of saying 'hello'?" said Alan.

"More like 'good-bye', Mr. Silverman," said Vitaly, grinning. "The world is reliant on the internet – for everything. Your phones, commerce, banking – it's all inter-connected."

"And secured in a number of different ways," added Wendy. "There's no way you'd break it all."

"Security," chuckled Vitaly. "What you call 'security' is a complete joke. Tell me you haven't seen the headlines. World corporations get hacked every day. Millions of credit card numbers and passwords are compromised in minutes in your 'secure' world – most of the time the target company does not even know it. There is not a single credit card anywhere in the world that I could not have access to in under an hour, if I so desired."

"You'd still have to break into hundreds and hundreds of systems," said Alan. "- that takes time."

"Break in?" said Vitaly, laughing out loud. "My dear man, they've all LET me in. As you no doubt are aware from your little visit to Symantec, all I need is already everywhere I need it."

"So you're going to block the DNS - - -again?" said Wendy.

"Who said block?" said Vitaly. "This time, I'm going to break it – for good. The world will be in economic chaos for months."

"That includes you," said Alan.

"On the contrary," said Vitaly. "I will be very well off – even after the smoke has cleared."

They all sat in silence for a moment. It was a lot to take in.

"Oh, and since I know you're already aware," said Vitaly, "- there will be no 'white knight' to rescue the internet. I'm fully aware of ICANN's fall-back plans – those egotistical fools even led me to the key holders - on their own website. I have what I need to prevent any heroics and I assure you, there is no garish and idiotic reset mechanism at this facility, like your friend Mr. Boyle has back in California."

Alan and Wendy looked at each other again. He knew what they knew.

"When does all of this happen?" said Alan.

"Since you are my guests and there is nothing you can do to stop it, there's no reason not to tell you," said Vitaly. "Tomorrow is my mother's birthday. She was killed - taken from me by the Russians a few months ago. To honor her and to honor all who've been lost, tomorrow is the day of reckoning."

He sat back down in his chair and swiveled around to face the monitors once again.

"Tomorrow," he said,"- is 'Apokalypsis'."

CHAPTER 35

Alan and Wendy were led out of Vitaly's office and escorted back to a set of conference rooms that had been turned into a makeshift holding area. It had been where Alan had been held the night before.

During their visit to Vitaly, the area had been cleaned and a second cot had been added. Sandwiches and hot tea had been set aside on the far counter. There was also a small bathroom with a shower and sink attached to the meeting space. Guards had been stationed outside the door, so there was no chance of attempting an escape.

"Welcome to my room," said Alan, "- looks like we'll be sharing today."

Wendy walked around the perimeter and stared up at the ceiling. She saw no monitoring devices, but assumed that someone somewhere was keeping an eye on them.

"I thought you were dead," she said, grabbing a cup of tea from the counter.

"I felt like it," Alan added, "- pavement is not fun to bounce around on."

"Did they interview you at all before I arrived?" she asked. "Any torture or questioning?"

"Nope," said Alan, "- just treated my wounds, gave me some Tylenol, then offered me a hot meal, shower, and a cot. I met with Lukashenko briefly when I first arrived. I thought I was done for. I was still a bit out of it from the accident. I fed him a lie about everyone back at the office already knowing what was up – he knew it was bogus. I was sure he was gonna have me taken out back and whacked, but they sent me here instead."

"He wanted to make sure of what I knew," said Wendy, "- and he used you for leverage."

"Sorry," said Alan, grabbing a sandwich and taking a bite. "I thought you'd have been long gone by now. Thanks for sticking around, though."

"At least we know we were right – Frank was too," she added.

"What about your hacker friend?" Alan asked. "Do you think he's made any headway?"

"I'd call him to find out," said Wendy sarcastically, "- but I seem to have been relieved of my phone."

"Well," said Alan, "- I'm fresh out of ideas, for the moment."

"Looks like we have some time to think about it," said Wendy. "Apparently, tomorrow is 'D-Day'. Until then, I guess there's nothing to do but wait."

"Yeah," said Alan. "I don't think we're going to miss the big show. Old Ponytail upstairs seems to want us to see what's up with his plan."

"You mean - watch everything go down, don't you?" said Wendy.

"World's biggest internet outage," said Alan. "One for the record books – you'll be able to tell your grand-kids about it - some day."

"So you'll be making a phone call to some little rascals right after this is over then, I take it?" she added.

"Nice," said Alan. They both smiled.

CHAPTER 36

Surprisingly, both Alan and Wendy had a restful night's sleep, in spite of the circumstances. They were roused by the guards early the next morning, took turns using the bathroom to freshen up and dress, and were each just finishing their morning coffee when they were summoned back to the Operations floor. Wendy was quickly finishing up a piece of fruit for her breakfast.

"Last meal?" said Alan.

"You want to die on an empty stomach?" Wendy replied, arching her brow at Alan.

"If I am to die in the morning, it'll probably happen that way," answered Alan. "I'm just a coffee man any time before noon. Honestly, with all of this traveling and excitement, my body doesn't know what time it is anymore."

"I'll second that emotion," said Wendy.

They were led back to the Operations Center, which was a hub of activity. Additional technicians had been brought on, and every monitoring station was manned – sometimes with two people. Wu Li Chang was quietly moving about the Operations floor, slowly looking over everything.

Alan and Wendy could see Vitaly Lukashenko in his office, which was situated above the Operations floor. He was also quietly looking over the scene, taking everything in.

The guards motioned for Alan and Wendy to move towards the stairs that led up to the office. They entered the glass office - the guards retreating after ensuring that Alan and Wendy reached their destination.

Vitaly was again wearing a perfectly tailored suit, this time pinstripe gray, which perfectly matched the color of his eyes. His hair was neatly pulled back into its usual blonde ponytail, and today he was sporting an expensive silver Amiga wristwatch. He did not turn to acknowledge Alan and Wendy's presence.

In the ensuing silence, Alan and Wendy also stared out at the Operations floor. There was a worldwide map up on the larger central screen, with smaller regional maps along both sides. Additional monitors were scrolling various kinds of data all over the far wall. A large digital clock was also posted above the world map. It currently read 08:47 AM.

After a few more seconds, Vitaly spoke.

"Thank you for that," he said.

"For what?" asked Wendy.

"For the silence," said Vitaly, "- for respecting the moment. Too often – at times like these, the impending sense of what is about to happen is ruined with thoughtless babble and banter."

"There's still time to change your mind," said Alan. "I don't understand what all of this will prove. You wreck the world's economies, but everyone – including you – will suffer for it. I don't see how this accomplishes you goals."

"You Americans," sniffed Vitaly, still not looking at them but staring out at the floor, "- you never see the big picture. The world economies are interested in only one thing – to make more money. Governments and corporations don't care about the damage they inflict or the people they destroy – it's all about the bottom line."

"I don't see how the Russian invasion of your homeland relates here," said Wendy.

"Of course you don't," said Vitaly. "You're not really interested because it DOESN'T relate to you. There is no gold, no technology, nothing to gain by stepping in to help my people. Your home – your family – goes about its daily routine. You buy your 'Starbucks' and watch your 'Netflix'. You say "oh, isn't that terrible what's happening over there" and couldn't even find it on a map if you were asked. So my solution is simple. I will create a level playing field. The governments and corporations of the world will spend their time sifting through the ashes of their age of consumption. They will have to react to the panic and calamity of their own people. We will ALL be equal – in terms of wealth and power. It will be glorious."

"You'll be broke as well," said Alan.

"I told you, my wealth has been shielded from the coming danger," said Vitaly.

"So you'll be the world's only rich man," said Alan, "- then what?"

"I will use my wealth to help my country," said Vitaly. "My fortune will be theirs. It will be used to rebuild. WE will be a "first world" nation in the new era - - - WE will lead."

"With you at its head, I assume," added Wendy.

"A movement and revolution needs a leader," said Vitaly. "I will gladly take the role I was destined for."

Alan looked at Wendy. It was clear, Vitaly was drunk with power. Enamored with his own ego and worldly aspirations, he spoke with the arrogance of a man who knew his way was the only way – and that his will was going to happen.

Alan glanced over at Vitaly's desk. Resting on it was a clear plastic box, fitted with four inserts. Sitting within each insert was an ordinary-looking card key. Each one had large, simple block lettering emblazoned on the card. From left to right the cards read "NUMBER 1", "NUMBER 3", NUMBER 5", and "NUMBER 6".

Alan nodded his head over in the desk's direction. Wendy looked over and saw the cards as well.

The four missing key-cards.

The key-cards that could reset the DNSSEC system and "reboot" the internet. Combined with the two already in the FBI/NSA's possession back in the states, they would have five out of the seven cards needed to reboot the system at ICANN headquarters.

It was just like Vitaly's personality to have them all on display, right out in the open. Surely, Vitaly knew that Alan and Wendy knew what they were. It added to the self-assuredness of the man who was now silently watching the clock over the world map in the Operations Center.

The clock read 08:54 AM, Hong Kong time.

"Its time," said Vitaly. He turned and motioned for Alan and Wendy to leave the office with him.

"Won't you join me?" he said, walking towards the door. "You're about to witness history."

CHAPTER 37

08:56 AM.

Vitaly took a position in the middle of the raised platform overlooking the entire Operations floor. Alan and Wendy were stationed off to one side, under the watchful eye of an armed escort. He held up his hand, and Wu Li Chang shouted a clipped order in Mandarin.

Everyone stopped working and turned towards Vitaly.

All was silent, except for the humming of fans and cooling systems.

"Ladies and gentlemen," he began, "- this is an historic day. It's the culmination of years of planning and work, much of which has been done by all of you. For that I thank you. One book is closing – a book of greed, corruption, self-righteous power, and oppression. A new one will be started today. Like the Phoenix, this new society will rise from the ashes of the old. The world is about to witness what happens when they ignore the weak and the helpless, as they themselves will become weak and helpless. To quote the Old Testament – 'an eye for an eye – a tooth for a tooth'. You all know your assignments. Execute them. You will be rewarded in the new society that starts today."

He looked at the clock on the wall.

08:59 AM.

He nodded at Wu Li, who shouted another order. The technicians all returned their attention to their stations.

"Let's begin," Vitaly said – to no one in particular.

The clock clicked over.

09:00 AM.

"For you mother," Vitaly whispered. He closed his eyes and gave the code word.

"Apokalypsis," he said, in a strong and confident voice.

CHAPTER 38

Alan and Wendy's attention was glued to the large monitors stationed on the far wall of the Command Center.

At first, it seemed like nothing was happening. The technicians were staring hard at their monitors, but nothing visible had changed on the screens at their stations or the large overhead maps. There were also monitors on the large wall of the Operations Center that showed various websites up and active. There was one for Alibaba, the Chinese e-commerce giant. There was one for TenCent Holding Limited, a mass media, phone service, and internet conglomerate based in Hong Kong (and the fifth largest internet company in the entire world). There was a screen showing activity on the Hong Kong Stock Exchange.

There were also displays showing companies that both Alan and Wendy were more familiar with, like Facebook Asia, Google Asia, and CNN-Asia.

Alan whispered out of the side of his mouth to Wendy without turning his head.

"We've got to do something," he said.

"What do you suggest?" she whispered back. "There's nothing we can do to stop the virus's impact now – he's activated it."

"What about the remaining key-cards in Vitaly's office?" said Alan, still whispering.

"OK," she said. "What about them? Even if we could grab them – then what? The facility to reset the DNSSEC protocol is half a world away."

One guard caught their whispering and motioned for them to be quiet. Everyone in the room was transfixed at the screens on the far wall – waiting.

The clock on the wall now read 09:07 AM.

Over the loudspeaker that could be heard across the entire Operations floor came Wu Li's voice.

"Penetration confirmed," he said.

"Where?" said Vitaly, speaking into a wireless headset he had mounted to his head. His voice came over the loudspeaker as well.

"'TenCent' Holdings Limited," said Wu Li. "They are beginning to lose connectivity at their Corporate Headquarters."

"Show me" said Vitaly.

A technician typed a few commands into his workstation keyboard. One of the outside screens flashed up to a network map of the Hong Kong Business District. A green dot on one of the buildings was beginning to slowly flash between green and red.

Vitaly smiled. It was finally beginning.

"Excellent," said Vitaly, "- I want to know when and where every large activation occurs."

"As you wish," said Wu Li.

CHAPTER 39

Frank Alvis had been a busy boy.

Ever since Wendy Tosca had put together the government's little arrangement with Frank following his long-ago break-in to the Pentagon's secure website, Frank had taken the precaution of monitoring Wendy's cellphone - totally unbeknownst to her, of course. Frank always believed it was useful to have access to something and not need it rather than need it and not have it. That's part of what the thrill of hacking was for Frank. It's true he did take advantage of some things for personal gain, but they were always trivial, like the hockey tickets. Frank would never even think of using his access and knowledge for real trouble.

This recent puzzle brought to him by Alan and Wendy had intrigued Frank, though. All the signs pointed to Hong Kong. Someone there was serious.

Breaking the internet. It would be the grand-daddy of all hacks.

Unless of course it could be stopped.

Stop the hack of all hacks? That would one-up anyone and add to the already legendary status for 'Tron007'. He was hooked from their first conversation. He had been devoting every waking hour preparing over the past week.

Anything he could get access to in the Asia-Pacific region — routers, switches, servers — you name it — Frank was looking for a way in. He had amassed an impressive list of accessible systems and equipment. He had slept very little over the past twenty-four hours, but his body was running on Red Bull and Cheetos. He was in the zone. If Wendy saw him now, she'd re-think the decision about not having him arrested on the spot.

But now — she needed him. What if the worst-case scenario he predicted was to actually happen?

The whole world would need him.

He had lost contact with Wendy's phone the previous day. Someone had turned it off, and he knew it wouldn't have been Wendy. He had tracked her to the Renaissance Harbour View Hotel in downtown Hong Kong, so he knew both her and her new partner, Alan, had to be close by.

All signs pointed to Hong Kong for the grand show-down, and that's where Frank was watching. Looking for anything suspicious.

He saw it shortly after 08:00 PM, Pittsburgh time.

Network connectivity was flapping at a building in the Hong Kong business district. He cross-referenced a map from another site, and saw that it belonged to TenCent Holding Limited, one of the largest content and service providers in the world - even though most in the US had never even heard of it.

At about 08:10 PM, the entire building had dropped. Outages were starting to fan out at buildings nearby.

Whatever was happening -it had begun. This had to be it.

"I see you," said Frank, smiling. He began furiously typing at his keyboard.

CHAPTER 40

Things were beginning to roll in Hong Kong.

Within twenty minutes, Alibaba, the huge e-commerce site based in China was starting to feel the effects of the virus. Their website was down. Little did the techs know at Alibaba, but it wasn't coming back up. Not for a long time.

The opening bell at the Hong Kong Stock Exchange had barely rung when their systems began fizzling out. Local news was showing traders - frantic to get their orders in and out - shouting, waving their arms, and running around in a panic. Fights were breaking out on the stock exchange floor. The news reports were stating there appeared to be a computer malfunction. That was a complete understatement.

Links on the Facebook Asia homepage were breaking, throwing back errors such as "page unavailable" or "file not found, please try again later."

Vitaly was calmly watching the chaos unfurl. He was sipping a cup of green tea from his perch high above the computer Operations floor.

Wendy and Alan felt helpless. A screen showing all of Hong Kong's data links was plastered on the far wall. It was slowly turning from all green to red, and picking up speed.

"Why aren't we losing connectivity here?" said Alan, puzzled.

"Because Vitaly and his team didn't download the virus," said Wendy. "Remember, it only destroys the links between the DNS table and the actual IP addresses, not the physical cables and connections themselves."

"So it's basically like a blind man in a china shop," he said. "All the expensive stuff is still there, it's just that the blind man can't see it."

"Or tell anyone where anything is," added Wendy.

"Of course," said Alan, "- no one knows that yet."

"Nope," said Wendy, "- right now everything is just getting crushed."

"Look at that," said Alan. "Google-Asia is starting to lose it."

She glanced over at the big board, looking at a side monitor that was displaying the Google-Asia homepage. It was now displaying a "page unavailable" screen.

"Unreal," she said, shaking her head.

In a few minutes, Wu Li's voice came over the loudspeaker again.

"Sir, we've detected a problem," he said.

"Problem?" said Vitaly, finishing his tea. "What problem?"

"The virus penetration seems to have halted moving out to the east," Wu Li said.

"What do you mean?" said Vitaly.

"The virus can't make the jump to the Japanese network over the Tokyo network link," said Wu Li. "The link has been severed at the switch level."

"Reroute it and continue," said Vitaly. "Go through the Bejing link instead."

"We're trying," said Wu Li, "- but those switches are being killed as well."

"Fix it, Wu," said Vitaly. His voice was beginning to rise.

Wu Li Chang took a deep breath and delivered the bad news.

"I can't," he said.

Wendy and Alan looked at each other and both knew almost instantly what was happening. They both mouthed the same word to each other, breaking into a slight smile.

"Frank!"

CHAPTER 41

Frank was in his glory.

It was the type of engagement Frank loved - fluid and mobile.

One on screen he was carefully watching the spread of the virus throughout the Hong Kong area. On a second, he had pulled up a map of the network links for all of Southeast Asia. On a third, he had pulled up tabs with various Asian Tel-com companies he had hacked in the previous twenty-four hours.

His plan was quite simple. He observed the point of origin for the virus, pulled back to a circle of about fifty to one-hundred miles, and was beginning to hack into the network switches and kill them, one by one. This would prevent the spread of any data - and the virus, containing the damage to a small, but manageable kill zone.

It was easier than it sounded. There were so many connections in and out of Hong Kong. Small data pipes led to larger data pipes, and they fed into massive relay stations that accessed all points of the globe.

First things first.

He killed the outgoing data links from Hong Kong that went to Midway Island in the Pacific. It didn't seem like a logical choice, but Midway linked into Hawaii, which linked into San Francisco.

San Francisco linked into everything in the continental United States.

Frank may have been a hacker, but he was also an American. Protect the house first – then help the neighbors.

After he killed the U.S. pipe, he concentrated on the big Asian gateways.

He next killed the Tokyo link.

He was talking to himself as he worked, anxious sweat rolling off of him.

"Oh no you don't!" he'd shout, watching the virus's progress by the changing color of the link from green to red. He'd then quickly enter commands on the corresponding Tel-com's system, ordering the local network switches to shut down.

He then went to work on the Bejing link.

Once that had been disabled, he started picking out smaller and smaller lines. He was like a sharpshooter, but barely one step ahead of the virus.

In another twenty minutes, it was done.

He had quarantined it all.

There was a large network death zone stretching out from Hong Kong for a distance of about seventy-five miles, but it went no further.

"Ha-ha!" screamed Frank, with a joyful fist raise of victory. "- I fart in your general direction!" he added, in a cheesy, French accent – an homage to one of his favorite 'Monty Python' movies .

"Your mother was a hamster, and your father smelled of elderberries!" He grabbed yet another can of RedBull and emptied it, tossing the can over his shoulder.

CHAPTER 42

Vitaly Lukashenko was absolutely furious. He was watching the red lines as they snaked outwards from Hong Kong. They had all suddenly stopped, as if something or someone was holding them back – preventing them from continuing their infection.

"Wu!" screamed an angry Vitaly. "What is happening?!?"

"It's the switch links sir," replied Wu Li, in a very calm and even voice. "They have been severed in a concentric circle just outside of the Hong Kong network."

"I don't understand," said Vitaly. "Fix it - - -fix it now!"

"There is nothing to fix," said Wu Li. "The switches have been deactivated at the source. We'd have to have access to the various local Tel-Coms and their network configuration set-ups to restart the switches. Someone on the outside has penetrated those systems and manually shut down all of the routers and switches. They have essentially contained our impact area."

Vitaly paced back and forth on the walkway in front of his office like a caged animal. All of his work – the planning, the preparation – all for naught. He glanced over at Alan and Wendy, who were still watching the monitors on the far wall.

"It was you!" he yelled, pointing a finger in both Alan and Wendy's direction.

Both Alan and Wendy acted surprised. They were indeed surprised at what they had just witnessed – and relieved. Frank had successfully stopped the spread of the virus – at least for now.

"You did this!" said Vitaly, repeating his accusation.

"How could we have done it?" asked Alan. "You've had us here – as your prisoners I might add – the whole time."

"You know what's going on," said Vitaly. He walked towards them, but stayed on his perch on the elevated platform.

"We don't," said Wendy.

"Liars!" yelled Vitaly, lashing out. He took a deep breath and smoothed his hair with his hand, trying to regain control of himself.

Alan and Wendy remained silent.

Vitaly had re-established his composure and was back to his well-rehearsed, cool exterior. He reached behind his back and pulled a nickel-plated revolver from his waistband. The entire room was now very, very tense.

"I am a man used to getting what I want," said Vitaly. "I do not accept failure."

He turned to the Operations floor. All eyes were on Viltaly and his brandished pistol.

"Wu Li," he calmly said. "I asked you to have these Americans eliminated. Now see what they have done?"

Wu Li Chang looked very nervous. He knew arguing with Vitaly would have been meaningless and would only further enrage him. He knew where the blame was going to be directed at now. He simply bowed his head in shame and acceptance.

"I hold you responsible, Wu," said Vitaly.

He slowly lowered his shiny revolver and calmly fired two shots. The first one missed completely and the second tore through Wu Li's shoulder. He spun around wildly and fell to the floor. He did not move any further. A small pool of blood could be seen forming next to his body.

The shock of the violence caused everyone in the data center to jump when the first shots were fired. There were also gasps of horror as Wu Li fell to the floor. The silence that followed was almost deafening. All that could be heard was the whir of the cooling systems in the data center as all of its living occupants held their collective breaths to see what would happen next.

Vitaly simply watched the body hit the ground and gave a sly smile, satisfied that at least one person would no longer disappoint him.

He turned to Alan and Wendy.

"And now you will undo what you have done," he said to them both.

"We've done nothing," said Alan. "Your plan failed – accept it."

"We shall see," said Vitaly.

He lowered his pistol again, this time pointing at both Alan and Wendy.

CHAPTER 43

Both Alan and Wendy froze as still as statues – eyes wide and afraid to move even a millimeter.

"Perhaps you need a better source of motivation," said Vitaly. He approached Wendy and grabbed her by the arm, twisting her around so that she was hugged up against his body. He lowered the pistol and placed it upon her temple.

"Stop it," said Alan. He held his arms outward towards Vitaly, pleading for him to cease what he was doing.

"I've already told you," said Alan, in a very calm and soothing voice, "- it wasn't us. We haven't done anything. Something else must have happened. Now why don't you put the gun down before someone else gets hurt?"

Vitlay chuckled a bit, still not releasing his grip nor changing his aim.

"Before someone else gets hurt?" said Vitaly. He laughed out loud. "Like whom? Ms. Tosca? What about the thousands of people in Crimea and the Ukraine – my people – who get hurt every day, hmmmm? Why don't you plead for them? This operation would have stopped their anguish. It would have diverted the Russians into looking after themselves instead of bullying others. It would have stopped my people's pain."

He looked over at the main monitoring screen again. The red lines still did not move from the concentric circle surrounding Hong Kong. Alan swore he saw a tear in the corner of Vitaly's eyes. The plan had failed.

Vitaly knew it.

Vitaly was also convinced that the Americans in front of him were somehow responsible for his grand plan's failure.

He looked back at Alan, re-adjusted his grip on his pistol - which was still pointed at Wendy's temple – and took a step back to give himself some room. He knew what he was going to do now.

"I will ask you one last time," said Vitaly, "- fix what you have broken, or Ms. Tosca dies."

Alan looked at Wendy, who seemed scared but calm. She gave Alan a look of anticipation - like something was about to happen.

Vitlay took another step back with Wendy in tow.

This time, Wendy suddenly took her left leg and stepped in behind Vitaly's backward movement. She swept it forward and ducked downward, using all of her weight to add to the force of its motion.

It caught Vitaly completely off guard. His gun-wielding hand flew up and out in the direction of Alan and the armed escort that was surrounding him. He was beginning to fall backwards.

Instinctively, but much too late, Vitaly pulled the trigger and the gun went off.

The shot ripped into the guard standing behind Alan on his right, striking him in the face and killing him instantly.

Wendy continued her tuck downward into a ball and now sprang from a crouched position into the falling Ukrainian. Both of his arms were in the air now, his body at a forty-five degree angle with the floor and falling rapidly.

Alan winced and ducked to his left at the shot, whirling around to smash his elbow into the chest of the guard behind him on his left. That man had been watching his partner's head explode from the errant shot from Vitaly. As he recoiled backwards from the force of Alan's sudden move, Alan reached downward and pulled the man's revolver from his holster.

Alan aimed upward and squeezed off two rounds, blasting through the man's chest as they both tumbled to the floor.

Vitaly hit the ground hard, the gun flying from his hand - rattling across the metal floor of the raised platform.

Wendy was on top of him now. She balled her hands together into a giant fist and came down hard on Vitaly's solar-plexus. The exhaling "oooooooffff" of the air exiting Lukashenko's lungs could be heard across the Operations floor.

Reflexively, Vitaly's legs rose from the blow, propelling Wendy over the top of Vitlay's head, spilling her onto the metal walkway. She landed hard, raised her head and continued to move forward, reaching out for the nickel-plated pistol that was on the floor in front of her.

Vitaly reached a free arm up, grabbing for Wendy's ankles. He clamped down on one and pulled hard, stopping her forward momentum.

She kicked hard with her free leg, catching him in the head. His grip loosened and she continued to scramble for the gun.

The data center had become a chaotic scene. Technicians were screaming from the shots and running in multiple directions to and fro across the Operations floor, trying to find an exit. People ran into each other and fell, only to be trampled by those behind them. Shouts of pain and moans of discomfort added to the pandemonium as the injured lay on the floor.

Wendy scrambled forward again, this time reaching the shiny pistol. She grabbed it and chambered a round, twirling to face her attacker.

Vitlay had flipped over and was scrambling after Wendy, closing in and reaching out to grab at her legs again.

She lowered the gun and promptly let loose a single shot.

The report echoed through the data center and there was more distant screaming.

Vitaly's forward movement had been completely halted, as if someone had physically grabbed him from behind. His face took on a look of complete surprise and he looked down.

The front of his grey pinstripe suit had a growing circle of crimson forming around his chest. He reached his hand towards his shirt and pulled it back out, inspecting his fingers. They were covered in blood.

He turned to Wendy, and in giant rush of adrenalin, he lunged at her one last time, unleashing a horrific scream.

Wendy fired twice more.

The bullets found their mark.

Vitlay twisted to one side, his eyes rolled up into the back of his head, and he landed – lifeless – on the metal walkway.

Vitaly Lukashenko, the mastermind and architect of this grand plan – was dead.

She slowly got to her feet, the Data Operations Center still a mass and frenzy of scattering bodies and noise, the technicians continuing to run for their lives.

She looked over at Alan, who was just rolling off of his dead guard. He sat on his behind and pulled his legs up, trying to catch his breath.

Wendy glanced over into the glass-enclosed office. She blinked and looked again, not believing what she was seeing

The box - the one on Lukashenko's desk in his office. The clear, plastic box containing the four key-cards was gone.

CHAPTER 44

Wendy was dumbfounded. Who could have slipped in and took the key-cards? Who even knew what they were? She yelled over to Alan, who was still regaining his wits about him.

"Alan!" she yelled. "The key-cards - - - they're gone!"

Alan's head shot up.

"What?!?" he replied. He glanced over towards the office and got to his feet.

"The case that had the missing key-cards," she repeated, "-it's missing from Vitaly's desk."

Alan darted his gaze around the room. His eyes came to the spot where Wu Li had been gunned by Lukashenko, just minutes earlier.

Wu Li Chang was gone.

Alan frantically ran towards the spot in the Operations Center where Wu had been, quickly scanning the floor to see if Wu had crawled behind one of the monitoring stations. He was nowhere to be found.

"Wendy!" Alan yelled, "- it's Wu Li Chang – he's gone!"

Now it was Wendy's turn to be surprised and shocked. She began scanning the room, looking for Wu Li.

Technicians were still frantically trying to get out of the building, running everywhere across the data center. Across the room, she could see the lobby area and the elevators. She could just make out a figure who looked like Wu Li, pushing his way into a full lift car, just as the doors closed behind him.

"The elevators," Wendy screamed. "He's headed for the parking deck."

Wendy dashed to the end of the raised metal platform, quickly navigated the stairs, and was headed for the stair exit at the far end of the room next to the elevator lobby. She suddenly stopped and turned to Alan.

"What floor was the parking garage on?" she shouted.

"What?" replied Alan, who was starting to make his way towards her.

"The parking garage," she said, waving her arms. "I was blindfolded when I was brought in – did you see the floor number when you were brought here?"

Alan looked skyward, trying to remember. It was all so fuzzy when he was dragged to the data center after his accident.

"I think it was Sub-Level 2 - - -no, it was Sub-Level 3!" he said.

"Are you sure?" she asked.

"No," he said. He tossed his pistol towards her. "Take this – you may need it."

She caught the gun in mid-air.

"Go – GO!" he yelled.

Wendy now had two weapons – the nickel-plated revolver that once belonged to Vitaly Lukashenko and the pistol that Alan had just thrown to her. She was checking the nickel-plated pistol as she ran towards the elevators. Only one shot left in that one.

She reached the elevator lobby and pushed her way past the milling technicians, reaching the door to the stairwell. She opened the door and began racing downwards.

She checked the other gun as she ran down. Four shots in that pistol – five shots total between the two weapons. She'd have to make them count, if she could even find Wu Li.

She rounded the landing that read "SUB-LEVEL 1". She was panting a little and bounding down the stairs, doing her best to take two at a time.

Round another turn and past the "SUB-LEVEL 2" sign. Only one more flight to go.

She reached the "SUB-LEVEL 3" landing and burst through the doors. The parking garage was busy here as well, with technicians escaping into their cars and racing towards the exit of the parking structure.

Two cars passed by Wendy. She pointed her weapon at the driver's side windows as each one passed by, but neither one was Wu Li. The second driver swerved to miss her, almost slamming into a concrete wall as the vehicle's tires wailed and screeched as it zoomed by.

Cars could be heard still driving on upper levels, their noise becoming fainter and fainter.

Then, there was silence.

If she had picked the wrong level, it was probably too late by now. She looked both left and right, trying to decide where to search first. She chose to go to her right, moving upwards towards the higher levels. If Wu Li was still in a level below her, he'd still have to pass her to get out of the building. She rounded the corner and was still making cursory looks into the parked cars.

Nothing.

She reached Sub-Level 2 and decided to go back the other way. Alan had guessed either Sub-Level 2 or Sub-Level 3 in his assumption on where he was brought in from. There was nothing on Sub-Level 2 that Wendy could see.

She systematically started searching the cars on the other side of the garage as she moved down through the parking level. She was using the pistol that Alan had thrown to her upon her exit, since it had more ammunition. She was sweeping the barrel across each vehicle, moving from one car to the next.

She could hear nothing now but her footsteps and her own heavy breathing.

Hope was fading rapidly. Wu Li Chang had given her the slip.

CHAPTER 45

Wu Li had taken the bullet to his shoulder, turned, and fell to the floor. He was not dead, but he dared not move for fear of another shot. He could feel the blood oozing from his shoulder, creating a puddle on the floor beside him.

Then he heard some additional shouting. More shots. Technicians around him began screaming and running. He finally had the courage to turn and look to see what was happening.

The Operations floor was a mad house. People were running everywhere, tripping over each other, trampling one another. People were lying on the ground, moaning in pain.

He looked up at the elevated platform. Vitaly and the woman were in a scuffle. To his right, the other American was also in a tussle with one of the guards.

Wu Li Chang knew of only one other play. He would retrieve the key-cards from Vitaly's office. It might buy him some leverage. He wasn't thinking straight – his shoulder ached, but he had to do something.

He quickly got to his feet and raced up the stairs and into Lukashenko's office. In one swoop he grabbed the clear plexi-glass container with the key-cards – one of them his own – and was back out of the door. As he came back down the stairs, he could see the American had the upper hand on his attacker. He heard two shots as he passed by and glanced over to see the guard's back exploding in blood and debris.

He heard more shots from the metal walkway. The crowd in front of him was impassable.

He turned to see Vitaly Lukashenko, the man who had publicly dishonored him, slump to the floor – dead. He was not sad to see him go.

He clutched the clear box a little tighter, turned towards the crowd, and began pushing his way towards an exit. The elevators were closer than the stairs, and the door had just opened up. People were piling in, and Wu Li joined them. He barely made it into the lift when the doors closed behind him.

He didn't know if the Americans had realized yet that he was gone. He felt a little better, but he'd feel much safer when he was back in his car and out of the building all together. He knew where Lukashenko's money was. He knew how to access it.

Wu Li Chang was now a rich man, and was just minutes away from disappearing for good.

He burst out of the elevator and ran towards his car, which was parked low on Sub-Level 3, almost to Sub-Level

4. He fumbled with the keys and slipped into the driver's seat.

He stopped to take a breath. His shoulder was really throbbing now, and he was dripping blood all over the car's interior. Pain shot through his whole arm if he tried to lift it. He would have to drive with only one hand.

He tossed the clear case with the key-cards onto the passenger seat. Wu Li then fumbled with the keys, almost dropping them before getting them into the ignition.

Then he froze.

He saw the American woman. She had emerged from the stair exit on Sub-Level 3. She was brandishing a weapon and looking around. He knew who she was looking for. By now they had figured out that he was not dead on the floor of the Operations Center and was gone – along with the key-cards.

Wu slumped down in his seat so just the top of his head was visible. Two cars passed the American woman. She pointed her pistol at each one - the second one nearly crashed.

Then there was silence.

The American woman began checking each car that was remaining, but she was moving up in the sub-levels, away from Wu. She disappeared from sight.

Wu Li had a decision to make. He would have to get by the American woman if he hoped to get out of the garage. He would have to take his chances – after all – he had a car, and she was only a woman.

He adjusted himself back up in the driver's seat and turned the ignition key, starting the car.

It was now or never for Wu Li Chang.

CHAPTER 46

Wendy heard the car start, almost a level below her.

She checked her weapon again. Four shots.

She also checked the nickel-plated pistol one more time. A single round. She laid it on the car hood beside her, stepped out into the parking garage's roadway, and waited.

She heard the car start moving. It was picking up speed rapidly.

It had to be him. It had to be Wu Li Chang.

She took a triangular stance and steadied herself, taking a deep breath to calm her nerves. She raised the weapon and prepared to fire.

Wu Li had his foot down hard on the accelerator, barely negotiating the tight turns inside the parking garage. He would build up plenty of speed and blow right by the girl – or over her – it didn't matter. He rounded the corner and saw her standing in the middle of the roadway. A gun was pointed at him.

Wendy saw the car turn the corner. Its lights were now on her. The driver was quickly swerving from side to side, trying to disorient her with the headlights. She began firing.

The windshield exploded.

The car continued towards her.

She emptied the clip on the pistol.

The car raged on, bearing down on her in the roadway.

Wu Li began swerving, hoping the light from his headlights would confuse the woman.

She opened fire.

The first shot caused the windshield to explode in ribbons of tiny glass fragments. Wu Li could barely see, but put his foot on the accelerator and pushed it to the floor. Shots continued to ring out, barely missing him as he drove.

Wendy had no choice.

She dove out of the way of the car, rolling to her right. As she came up, she grabbed the shiny pistol from the hood of the car, took aim, and fired her last remaining shot.

Wu Li saw the woman rolling off to the side as he passed. He smiled to himself. He was sure he had made it. Then, for some strange reason, he heard the rear windshield shatter. The back of his head felt warm. What a strange feeling – he felt like he was passing out. Consciousness instantly left him. He slumped forward in the car – dead before he hit the wheel.

Wendy saw the car swerve uncontrollably. It smashed into the wall and she heard air bags go off. She ran to the driver's side. Smoke from the deployed airbags filled the air. In the front seat, she could see Wu Li Chang, slumped forward on the driver's side airbag. The back of his skull had been blown open. He was looking at her – a blank look of surprise on his face.

Wu Li Chang was dead.

Wendy could smell the gasoline and feared that the car might explode into flames at any moment. She looked past Wu into the passenger seat.

On the floor of the passenger side she saw it - - the clear plexi-glass case with the four key-cards.

She ran around to the passenger side of the car and tried the door. It was jammed. She took the nickel-plated pistol, turned it around butt-first, and smashed in the window. She cleared the shards of glass out of the way and leaned into the car, grabbing the case.

Vitaly Lukashenko was dead.

Wu Li Chang was dead.

The virus had been stopped.

Wendy was holding the remaining DNSSEC reboot cards in her hand.

It had been a busy morning.

CHAPTER 47

Alan was slowly walking around the data center, trying to comfort the wounded and help where he could. He looked up at the monitors on the far wall. The virus still appeared to be contained, and was still only impacting a concentric circle in and around the Hong Kong area.

Local law enforcement and medical assistance was also starting to arrive. Alan was now busy showing his badge around and trying to give brief descriptions as to what had happened, who the main players were, and why he was there. There were a lot of angry looks and gestures from the local authorities, which was to be expected.

Alan was still talking to a police official when he saw Wendy walking back in from the elevator lobby. She caught his attention and held up the plexi-glass case which contained the four missing key-cards. Alan smiled at her, excused himself from his conversation at hand, and came over to her.

"Are you all right?" he asked.

"I'll be OK," she said with a slight smile.

"And Wu Li?" continued Alan. He thought he already knew the answer.

"He won't be joining us – or anyone else – from now on," she added, sitting down in one of the technician's chairs.

Alan patted her on the back.

"We should try to contact Frank," said Alan, "- see what's going on from his end."

Wendy realized that in all of the most recent confusion, she had completely forgotten about Frank. She had forgotten about the man who had basically foiled the entire plot. She had to speak with him.

"Where are those two guards that were with you?" she said, jumping up from her chair.

"Over there," said Alan, puzzled at the question.

Wendy looked over to see a medical team lifting up one of the bodies and laying it on a stretcher, getting ready to remove it from the scene.

"Wait, Wait!" shouted Wendy, looking in the direction of the EMTs. "*Dendai! – Dendai!!!*" she shouted again, this time so they would understand her.

The technicians both looked over at Wendy. She flashed her badge and motioned for them to hold for a moment.

She ran her hands down both sides of the dead guard, feeling for his pockets. She felt the hard lump on the left side, and retrieved what she was looking for.

Her cellphone, which had been taken away from her at the hotel.

"Thank you – *Xie-Xie*," she said to the team, bowing. They returned her bow and carried on, rolling the stretcher out of the Operations area and towards the elevators.

She flicked the phone on and it powered up. She was beginning to look up Frank's number when the cell phone rang on her end.

"Speak of the devil," said Wendy.

"Where have you been?" asked Frank Alvis, on the other end of the line.

CHAPTER 48

"We've had a busy morning, Frank," said Wendy. You could almost hear the excitement in her voice. "I see you have as well."

"Are you and the old geezer OK?" asked Frank.

Wendy laughed, looking over at Alan and mouthing the words "Frank" towards him as she pointed at the phone. Alan nodded and smiled.

"We're fine," said Wendy. "Frank, you've done a great job. I could kiss you."

Frank blushed on his end of the line.

"The threat here has been neutralized – and thanks to you, the spread of the virus has been contained.

"Only temporarily," said Frank. "We have to keep the network links down or else the virus will pick right back up where it left off. The virus has to be killed from the source."

Wendy looked up at the monitoring screens. She could see the big companies that were currently down.

'TenCent' Holding Limited – Alibaba - the Hong Kong Stock Exchange. Though they had limited the damage of the Apokalypsis virus, even at this level, there was going to be worldwide economic impact.

There was still work to do.

She had an idea.

"Frank, how long can you keep the network links down?" she asked.

"As long as you want," said Frank. "I'll need to go in and knock out any access to the Chinese Tel-Com systems – or else their personnel will try to log-on and turn them back on, thinking they are doing the right thing."

"Do it," she said, "- and keep them off – at least until I tell you otherwise."

"Done," he said.

"I'll be in touch," said Wendy.

She hung up the phone and walked over to Alan.

"How's our boy?" he asked.

"In his glory," Wendy replied. "He's going to make sure that no one from the Tel-Com companies can go in and release the network blockages. That'll keep the virus contained for now."

"Good," said Alan. "What's next?"

She tossed Alan the phone.

"Call ICANN," she said, "- and get your friend Martin Boyle on the phone."

CHAPTER 49

Martin Boyle was sitting in his apartment at 07:00 PM. He was at his desk reviewing some papers when the phone rang. He checked the number on his caller-ID, but didn't recognize it. Hoping he wasn't going to be faced with yet another blunt conversation with a tele-marketer, he answered.

"Hello," said Martin.

"Martin, its Alan Silverman," said Alan.

"Alan!" said Martin. "How nice of you to call. How's – "

"Martin, listen to me," interrupted Alan, "- we've had a situation and we need your help."

Martin quickly understood the gravity of Alan's tone and went from cheerful to serious.

"I'm listening," he said.

Alan sighed. Where to begin?

"OK – first, my partner Wendy and I are in Hong Kong," said Alan.

"Hong Kong?" said Martin.

"Yes," said Alan. "There's been an incident. A virus was released that took down a bunch of companies over here."

"Was it that DNS scenario we were discussing on your last visit?" said Martin.

"Yes," said Alan. "The virus has destroyed the tables that resolve the local DNS to the IP addresses for hundreds of machines here in Hong Kong. They've been completely wiped out – no auto-fix this time."

"Dear lord," said Martin. "Is it still spreading? Has it been contained? This is bad, Alan – this is very, very bad." Martin was standing up now and beginning to pace around his apartment. He understood what this could mean.

"Martin, I want you to calm down," said Alan. "We have contained the damage – for the moment."

Martin let out a sigh of relief.

"But," said Alan, "- there is still a danger.

"Give me the details," said Martin.

"We've had some help," said Alan, "– from the outside. Our man has shut off all of the network links in an area outside of Hong Kong, so the damage has been contained."

"Smart thinking," said Martin.

"Yes," said Alan. "Our guy knows his stuff. The problem is – "

"The problem is - ," interrupted Martin, "- that you've only temporarily contained the virus. If someone releases the network links, the virus will pick right back up where it left off."

"Exactly," said Alan. "We need your help. We need to reset the DNSSEC for Hong Kong, rebooting the system with the device you showed us back in California."

"Alan," said Martin. "I'm sorry, but like I explained to you when you were here, without at least five of the seven key-cards, we won't have enough of the encrypted code to perform the reset. We've only got two."

"Correction," said Alan. "We've got six now."

"What?" said Martin. "Wait – how?"

"Never mind that now," said Alan. "The point is with your two cards and our four, we have enough to reset the system, am I correct?"

"Of course," said Martin, "- but the reset machine is here in California – the problem is in Hong Kong – and your problem is localized. The system here is designed to reboot everything – worldwide."

"Can't you come up with some sort of portable system?" asked Alan.

Martin thought for a moment. The idea of using the reboot emergency scenario in a localized environment had never been on their minds at ICANN when they designed the fail-safe. He was quickly reviewing the set-up in his head.

"There may be a way," said Martin. "It's never been tried before – I can't guarantee it will work."

"We'll have to take that chance," said Alan. "How soon can you be in Hong Kong?"

"What?" said Martin.

"Grab your key-cards and anything you need," said Alan. "Bring whomever you need. We need you here – now."

"I'll be there as soon as I can," said Martin. His mind was already whirling, trying to develop his theory.

"The sooner the better," said Alan.

He hung up the phone.

"Well?" said Wendy.

"Well," said Alan, "- now we wait."

"And cross our fingers," added Wendy.

Alan nodded, rolling his eyes.

CHAPTER 50

It was probably the longest eighteen hours of their lives.

Alan and Wendy had squared everything away with the local law enforcement authorities. The data center had been cleared of the injured and the dead, and they had checked back in at both FBI and NSA headquarters, updating their status and the current situation.

Martin and a team of programmers were in-flight, so there was nothing to do now but wait.

Both Alan and Wendy finally got some food and some rest back at the Renaissance Harbour View Hotel.

It was around 05:00 AM the next day when they arrived back at the data center.

It was a different scene all together than when they had been here before.

The room was the same, all the monitors still showed their various status screens, and there was still the large map up showing the red dots and lines indicating the dead and/or non-working data links in the Hong Kong area.

The difference this time was in the personnel.

Every company that had felt the impact of the outage had their own field teams onsite now. 'TenCent' Holding

Limited had their team, Alibaba had another – there was one for the Hong Kong Stock Exchange as well. In all, over twenty-five internet companies and other computer-based companies were represented. Each field team had taken over one of the various monitoring stations that dotted the Command Center floor.

There was, of course, bickering and shouting going on. Lots of hand waving and raised voices as each team tried to assert their dominance and importance.

Alan and Wendy headed up to Vitaly Lukashenko's old office, which was now being used as an overall war-room for the issue. Vitaly's desk had been replaced with a large conference table.

Here too, were representatives from the various companies. These were the executives, who were also arguing over various points. In the far corner was a frazzled CIA field agent, who had been tasked with keeping the peace until Alan and Wendy arrived. The look on his face told the whole story.

"Good morning," said Wendy. "I'm Agent Wendy Tosca, from the NSA, this is Agent Alan Silverman from the FBI." They flashed their badges to confirm their identities.

"Shen Li Quong," said the man, in perfect English. He extended his hand.

"How long have they been like this?" said Alan, gesturing towards the executives in the conference room.

"Since the beginning," said Shen, "- some of them have been here for hours. They all want to run the show their own way. I've been just trying to tune them out. They stopped yelling at me just before you arrived, so be careful."

"Why is that?" said Wendy.

"Fresh meat," said Shen. "Don't worry, they are all going to tell you how important they are and why they should be helped first. They are sizing you up now." He nodded his head as he looked over at the assembled executives.

Some were pointing over at Wendy and Alan. Some were whispering among themselves.

"I see," said Wendy.

"We'll take it from here, Shen," said Alan. "Take a break, go get some coffee or tea – hell, just take a break from the noise."

"Gladly," said Shen, smiling. "They are all yours."

Wendy and Alan looked quickly left.

"You do the talking," whispered Wendy, "- you know how these execs over here are with women."

"Gee, thanks," said Alan.

They moved to the center of the table, Wendy taking a step back to stand behind Alan, telling all the men there by her body language that he was in charge.

Gentlemen," he began. "My name is Agent Alan Sliverman of the FBI. This is my partner, Wendy Tosca of the NSA."

Wendy bowed.

"I know you have been briefed," said Alan, "- rest assured that we are doing all we can. At the moment, we are waiting the arrival of a technical team from the ICANN institute in California. They should be arriving very shortly. Once they are here we are going to attempt a solution to the current situation at hand."

"Situation?" said the executive from Alibaba. "That's an understatement. Do you realize the revenue we are losing right now? Every second we wait costs us money! We must do something now!"

Other heads nodded in agreement.

"There is nothing that can be done at the moment," said Alan, trying to calm the crowd. "I must also emphasize that the ICANN resolution plan is theoretical one."

"Theoretical!" screamed the 'TenCent' Holding Limited Executive. "You mean you don't even know if it will work?"

"There is a chance that it will not," replied Alan, "- that is correct."

There was more murmuring and arguing between the executives. After a minute or so, Alan held up his hands to quiet down the crowd.

"The only other alternative I can advise you on is the worst case scenario," said Alan.

"Which is?" said the executive from the Hong Kong Stock Exchange.

"You will have to manually rebuild your DNS resolution tables – one machine at a time," said Alan.

"That could take weeks!" said one executive. "We'll be ruined!"

"This is unacceptable!" shouted another, "- there must be another way!"

"I'm sorry," said Alan. "This appears to be the only viable solution at the present moment."

"Mr. Silverman," said the Alibaba executive. "IF your plan is successful, in what order are we bringing the sites back up? Obviously, our company would want a higher priority – "

"That's absurd!" interrupted the Hong Kong Stock Exchange executive. "A retail site is high priority? Without the Stock Exchange, the entire economy is in jeopardy! WE should have priority!"

"My company will not take a back seat to yours!" shouted the 'TenCent' executive.

"Communications should be restored first!" shouted a cable executive.

The shouts across the table soon became unintelligible, as the executives continued to wave their arms and frantically argue.

Alan was trying to calm everyone down, but was not having any success.

Suddenly, Wendy jumped up on a chair and walked out onto the conference table. When she reached the center, she put two fingers to her lips and let loose a screeching whistle.

"Quiet!!!!!!!" she shouted. A few executives stopped talking, but most ignored her.

"Anjing – Anjing!!!!!" she shouted again, this time in Mandarin. She slammed her foot down hard on the table as well for greater effect.

The arguing executives were totally in shock. The American woman was making a spectacle of herself on the table. It did; however, have the desired effect. The room became quickly quiet as they all stared at the strange, whistling woman.

She motioned their attention back to Alan.

"Thank you," he said to Wendy, smiling at her.

"Of course," she replied. He helped her down from the table.

"Now," he said. "If the proposed solution works, all of the DNSSEC infrastructure should be reset, so there will be no need to prioritize. You should all be able to come back online together. Once the system has been reset, you can then – as individual organizations - take whatever steps you need to in order to restore your systems."

"What about the downed switches that are creating the current network blockage?" asked one executive.

"The blocks stay in place for now," said Alan. "It is currently the only thing that is preventing the further spread of the virus. If we can confirm that our proposed solution works, we can open the gates."

"And if not?" asked an executive.

"Then it's back to a manual rebuild," said Alan, "- or go out of business. Those will be your only options."

The gravity of that option was beginning to sink in on the assembled executives.

"What about the virus?" asked another executive. "It's still out there, isn't it?"

"It is," said Alan. "That's another reason we cannot open up the network. The downed devices are the only thing spreading the activation code of the virus to the rest of the internet – the worldwide internet. For now, we are concentrating on the problem before us, gentlemen – your problem."

Things were now not as combative. Some of the assembled men were now starting to nod their heads in agreement.

"When is the ICANN team due to arrive?" asked the Hong Kong Stock Exchange executive.

Alan looked at the clock on the wall. It was 06:00 AM, Hong Kong time.

"We hope to see them very soon," said Alan. "Their flight should have landed by now – they've been flown in by private jet, so there will be less time dealing with any airport delays."

There was more murmuring among the conference room.

"That's all for now," said Alan. "We'll keep you informed."

Alan thought he may have heard a "thank you" from the crowd, but he and Wendy retreated to one side of the room. The discussion among some of the executives resumed, but the crowd began to break up. Some of the company leaders went out into the data center to update their teams. Some sat back down to patiently wait. It was all they could do for now.

"Thanks for the help," said Alan.

"You looked like you needed a diversion," said Wendy. They both chuckled.

Wendy's cell phone began to ring. She answered it and handed it over to Alan.

"It's for you," she said. He took the phone.

"Yes?" said Alan.

"Alan? Martin. We've just landed. We'll be at your location in twenty minutes."

"Good," said Alan, "- the sooner the better."

CHAPTER 51

True to his word, in twenty minutes, Martin Boyle and his team arrived at the data center. Martin had brought three technicians with him, and each carried a large suitcase on wheels.

Alan strode across the data center floor to greet them.

"Martin!" exclaimed Alan, extending his hand. "Am I glad to see you!"

"Alan," said Martin, returning the handshake and giving Alan a smile. He looked around the room at all of the faces trained on his arrival. It made him more than self-conscious.

"I see we have a fan club," said Martin.

"They're your fans now," said Alan. "By the end of the day, they could be worse – if things don't go our way."

"We'll see," said Martin. "Where do you what my guys to set up?"

"Tell me what you need," said Alan.

"I'm going to need a large table for our equipment – somewhere close to a network connection so I can plug in," said Martin.

"Done," said Alan, and he hurried off to find a table.

Wendy came up to greet Martin.

"Ms. Tosca," said Martin, "- so good to see you again."

"I was just about to say the same thing to you," she replied. "Do you need anything from me at the moment?"

As a matter of fact," said Martin. "I do."

"Name it," said Wendy.

"Your network hero," said Martin, "- the one who successfully stopped the spread of the virus. Is there any way we could talk to him during this process?"

"I'll see what I can do," she said smiling.

"Excellent," said Martin. "Ahhh, here comes Alan with our table."

Alan came back into the Operations area on one end of a large table. Two of the internet executives were on the other end, and they placed it near one of the monitoring stations.

Martin turned to his team, who had been patiently waiting.

"Right here, boys," said Martin, pointing at the table. "Set it up, please."

He stepped away and the three-man team got to work, unpacking their cases and transferring equipment to the table. Alan motioned Martin over for a private conversation.

"First of all, smile and nod as if we're talking about something personal," said Alan, in a whisper.

Martin smiled and nodded.

"Is this going to work?" said Alan.

"We have no idea," said Martin, still smiling and nodding.

"That's not very reassuring," said Alan.

"We jumped on a plane as soon as you called," said Martin. "The fail-safe system was designed to work on a global scale – we have no idea what it will do when it's localized. My team was coding on the plane ride over. We've uploaded it into our portable system, but have no way of knowing if it will work."

"So it hasn't even been tested?" said Alan, trying hard to remain smiling.

"We're about to," said Martin.

"Wonderful," said Alan, patting Martin on the back.

Martin went back to the table to help his techs. Wendy was coming back across the room with a conference room speaker in one hand.

"What's that for?" asked Alan.

"Martin wants to talk to Frank when we get rolling," said Wendy. She looked over at the techs who were stringing cable seemingly everywhere. "This gonna work?"

"I wish I could tell you 'yes'," said Alan, "- but I'd be lying."

"Well, thank you, Professor Positive," said Wendy. She continued over to the table and hooked up the conferencing speaker.

In another thirty minutes, the techs were ready. The table was set-up similar to the mechanism back in California. Seven slotted card readers were positioned around a circular hub, each wired into a central processor. On the top of the processor was a large red button. A small monitoring screen was connected into the central processor, and it was currently showing a blank screen with a blinking cursor button in the upper left corner.

"OK," said Martin, "- we're ready to talk to your network guru. Who is this guy?"

"Actually," said Wendy, "- he's technically NOT a network guy. He works a bit in the shadows – you may know him as 'Tron007'."

"'Tron007'?" said Martin, a bit surprised. "You mean – as in 'Tron007' the hacker?"

"You've heard of him?" asked Wendy.

"Heard of him?" said Martin. "I'm surprised you haven't locked that guy up and thrown away the key. He's broken into our system many, many times."

"Done any damage when he was in there?" asked Wendy.

"Well - - no," said Martin.

"Which is why he is still on the outside," said Wendy. "He helps us, from time to time. He's the one who halted the advance of this virus."

"Impressive," said Martin, looking up at the network map of Hong Kong on the large monitoring screen on the far wall. The diagram still showed a large red circular spider-web of network connections that ended at various points around the outskirts of the city.

Wendy dialed up the phone.

"Frank, this is Wendy. Listen Frank, I need to put you on the speaker phone. We have some teams here that will need to interface with you."

There was some hesitance in the background.

"Please Frank," said Wendy. "You can trust me."

She nodded over to Alan, who turned on the speaker phone.

Wendy lowered her phone and spoke out loud.

"Frank, can you hear me?" she asked.

"I hear you," said Frank. His voice rang loud and clear through the box.

"Frank, we're here with Martin Boyle from ICANN," said Wendy. "He has a team here ready to try and reboot the DNSSEC system within your consolidated dead zone."

"Hello, 'Tron007'," said Martin. "It's nice to finally meet you. I must say I'm impressed with what you've done here thus far."

Frank smiled back in Pittsburgh. The reference to his cyber nick-name helped calm him down and ease the tension.

"Thank you," he simply said.

"How are the network blockages holding up?" said Wendy.

"So far so good," said Frank. "I've had a few attempts to bring some switches back online. It's not malicious – just employees from the local Tel-Coms trying to fix the system, which is only natural. I've been killing users on the system when I see them. The border is holding."

"That's great, Frank," said Wendy. "Thank you."

"So we're ready, then?" asked Martin.

"Looks like it," said Wendy.

"Let's do this," said Frank.

CHAPTER 52

"The key-cards, if you please," said Martin.

Wendy turned over the plexi-glass case with the four key-cards in her possession. Cards clearly labeled "NUMBER 1", "NUMBER 3", "NUMBER 5", and "NUMBER 6" could be seen through the clear carrying case.

Martin placed the case on the table and pulled the cards out, laying them neatly in order on the table in front of him. He turned to one of his technicians.

"Tony, our cards, if you please?" he said to the tech.

The technician pulled out two cards of his own. Each one was clearly labeled "NUMBER 2" and "NUMBER 7". Martin placed the cards on the table with the others, careful to put them in their proper order.

"I see we're missing number four," said Alan. "Is that going to be a problem?"

"We only need five out of the seven cards to physically reboot the system," said Martin. "We implanted a portion of the full code onto each of the cards, with enough overlap that only five would ever be needed to initiate a full restart. If we have more keys or are missing one of the cards in sequence, it doesn't matter."

"Because the overlap of code will still provide a full sequence?" asked Alan.

"Exactly," said Martin, nodding. "We do; however, have to read the cards into the system in their proper order or else the code is garbled."

Alan nodded back.

"Gentlemen," said Martin, "- are we ready?

"System is online and ready," said one technician. The technicians were all hunched over the small monitoring screen attached to the central processor.

"Code sequencer is active and ready," said a second.

Martin nodded. "'Tron007', is the network still holding?" he asked the speaker phone.

"Link stops are holding," said the voice from the phone.

The data center was as silent as Alan and Wendy had ever heard it. There were twice as many people jammed onto the Operations floor as there normally would have been. The various corporate executives lined the railing of the elevated platform. All eyes were on the large table with Martin's equipment and team surrounding it.

"Cross your fingers everyone – here we go," said Martin.

He picked up the key-card labeled "NUMBER 1".

"Initiating code re-assembly – section one", he said. He placed the key-card into the first card reader, which was located at about the two o'clock position on a clock face. The card reader flashed for a moment, then went green.

"Section one has successfully loaded," said one of the technicians.

Martin picked up the key-card labeled "NUMBER 2".

"Initiating code re-assembly – section two," he said. He placed the second key-card into the second card reader, which was located next to the first one. This card reader flashed longer than the first one, then finally turned green as well.

"Section two has successfully loaded," responded the technician. "Code merge is also complete and green."

Martin nodded. He picked up the key-card labeled "NUMBER 3".

"Initiating code re-assembly – section three," he said. Hey placed the third key-card into the third card reader. This card reader flashed even longer than the first two.

"Is there a problem?" asked Alan.

"No," said Martin. "Each section takes longer to add in and assimilate. If there is an issue, the key-card reader will turn red."

In a few more moments, the card reader went green.

"Section three," said the technician, "– loaded and code merge complete."

Martin nodded. He picked up the key-card labeled "NUMBER 5".

"Initiating code re-assembly – section five," said Martin. He skipped over the fourth card reader and placed the card labeled "NUMBER 5" into the fifth card reader slot.

"This one will tell the tale," said Martin. "It may take longer to merge this piece of code, since the fourth card was missing."

The card reader flashed and flashed for almost thirty seconds. All eyes in the room were staring at the reader.

It turned green.

"Section five," said the technician, "- has successfully loaded. The code merge is also complete and green."

Alan let out an audible sigh of relief.

Martin picked up the key-card labeled "NUMBER 6".

"Initiating code re-assembly – section six," he said. He placed the key-card into the sixth reader.

The reader flashed for almost forty-five seconds this time. It was nerve racking.

Suddenly, there were gasps heard from around the room.

The card reader did not turn green.

Instead, it turned a crimson red.

CHAPTER 53

Murmurs were beginning to be heard across the room. The key-card reader in the sixth position stayed red.

"What happened?" said Wendy.

Martin looked over at his technicians.

"Card six has been damaged somehow," said the technician. "It can't be read into the system."

The crowd noise began to grow louder. Panic was beginning to sweep the room. Martin held out his hands, begging for quiet.

"Calm down, everyone – please – calm down," he said. "This is why we only need five out of the seven cards to initiate a reboot. We're fortunate enough to have six with us today. We still have a chance for success."

"And if this last card doesn't work?" said Alan.

Martin didn't answer. Everyone in the room knew the answer.

Martin carefully reached out and picked up the card labeled "NUMBER 7".

"Initiating code re-assembly – section seven," he said. He slowly and deliberately placed the key-card into the seventh reader.

"Lucky number seven," murmured Alan.

"Let's hope so," whispered Wendy, who was standing beside him.

The card reader began flashing. It continued to pulse. The entire room was leaning forward, holding its collective breath. It seemed as if no one even dared to blink.

Forty-five seconds.

Still flashing.

One minute passed.

Still flashing.

One minute and twelve seconds.

The card reader went green.

One of the executives on the platform actually cheered out loud. Embarrassed, he lowered his head as order returned to the room.

All eyes were now on the technicians monitoring the central processing unit.

In a few moments, all of the techs looked up. One was smiling.

"Code re-assembly complete," he said, "- execution on your mark."

The central red button lit up. The system was ready.

"Here we go," said Martin.

He closed his eyes and pressed the button.

CHAPTER 54

The room once again held its collective breath.

The silence was broken by one of the ICANN technicians, who was monitoring the system on their small screen attached to the central processing unit.

"Executing DNSSEC reboot sequence," said one of the technicians.

At each individual monitoring station, the visiting emergency teams were also hunched over their own screens, looking for any signs of life for their individual systems. The rest of the room was glued to the large monitoring screens at the far end of the data center, which showed the large map of the Hong Kong area.

Alan crept up behind Martin.

"How long will this take?" whispered Alan.

"We have no idea," said Martin. "Remember, this is all theoretical. We've never had to actually perform a large-scale reboot before."

"You're a very reassuring guy," whispered Alan.

"Have patience," said Martin, still watching the main monitor, "- and have a little faith."

The ICANN technicians spoke up again.

"Initial reboot sequence appears to be successful. The code is self-replicating and distributing out across the system now."

One of the technicians from the Alibaba monitoring station began shouting.

"*Ta laile! – Ta laile!!!*" he shouted.

Alan and Martin looked over to Wendy.

She smiled.

"He says it's coming up!" she replied.

The same cry also came out from the Hong Kong Stock Exchange monitoring station. Then the TenCent Holdings station.

On the large monitor at the far end of the room, it was also now visible.

Green lines were taking the place of the red ones. They were slowly starting to fan out from the location of the data center.

The executives standing along the rail were audibly excited. They began shouting and waving their arms.

It was working. The system was slowly coming back up.

Martin, who up to this point had holding in his emotions, gave out a war-whoop of glee. He actually jumped up off of the ground and threw his fist in the air.

"Yesssss!!!!!" he shouted.

Alan's shoulders slumped forward in relief.

Wendy spoke into the speaker phone.

"Frank, are you seeing this?" she asked.

"Yup," said Frank. "All the systems are coming back online – looking good."

There was hand shaking, back slapping, an even the occasional hug springing up around the room.

In another fifteen minutes, the green lines had reached the network barrier that Frank had previously set-up.

Wendy, Alan, and Martin were still not celebrating. There was still one big hurdle left.

"Frank," said Wendy, "- we've reached your network plugs. Are you ready to open up a hole to see what happens?"

"I am," he replied. "I'm going bring up the Hong Kong link to a small data pipe –the one from Hong Kong to Macau. If we see any of those links go down, I can re-bottled it on the far end. There's only two ways in or out of that geography.

"OK," said Wendy. Both Alan and Martin were closely watching the big monitor.

"Here we go," said Frank.

The link stayed green.

"Is it open?" asked Wendy.

"Open and transmitting," said Frank. "Nothing is dropping in Macau. I think we've got it."

Now Wendy, Alan, and Martin could relax. The activation code word for the virus had been killed and the virus was not initiating on the far side of the network barrier.

"Open them all up, Frank," said Wendy. "I think we've done it." She was beaming.

In another three hours, all the monitoring stations were reporting good communication between all of their servers.

Alan and Wendy were sitting alone in the makeshift conference room – Vitaly Lukashenko's former office.

Martin Boyle came in. He was holding a bottle of champagne.

"Where did you get that?" asked Alan.

"I brought it along – just in case," said Martin, smiling. "Care to join me?"

"Absolutely!" said Wendy.

She found three crystal glasses in Vitaly's bar area.

Martin popped the cork and began filling the glasses.

"You know that virus that was implanted in the code is still distributed and out there," said Alan. "There's still a risk it could be re-activated – even accidentally."

"I spoke to Frank about that," said Wendy. "Turns out, he's been able to isolate exactly what the virus was and what the code did. He's already passed his findings along to Symantec. They can create a patch that essentially kills the malicious code and they can distribute it worldwide. Symantec says they'll have the patch ready tomorrow evening for delivery."

"Your hacker friend is turning legit," said Alan, taking a glass of champagne from Martin.

"I doubt it," said Wendy, also taking a glass. "He just likes being a hero now and again."

"What about you, Martin?" asked Alan. "What has ICANN learned about this whole experience?"

Oh - - nothing," said Martin, rolling his eyes. "Actually, we have some protocols and procedures to revisit. We've also learned the hard way that sometimes it pays to keep our big mouths shut, no matter what a publicist or over-eager exec might say."

"To lessons learned," said Wendy, raising her glass.

"To lessons learned," said Martin.

"Here, here," said Alan.

They touched their glasses together and took a long sip of champagne.

"And now I get to look forward to another fifteen hour flight and a mountain of paperwork," said Alan.

"You're such an old geezer," said Wendy.

Alan shot Wendy a nasty look, and then his face softened and he laughed out loud.

"There are days," said Alan, taking another sip of his drink. "There are days………."

THE END

Author Notes

Thanks for reading my book! If you enjoyed it, I hope you'll take the time to write a review of it at your favorite online retailer. Look for more titles from me in the future!

For those of you who may be wondering "did he make up this whole thing?" the answer is a resounding "no".

- Yes, there is an organization called ICANN
- Yes, they do have a DNSSEC reboot plan as a fail-safe plan that involves seven coded key-cards
- Yes, those cards are spread out around the world and in the hands of various individuals.
- Yes, the names of those key-card holders is published
- Yes, all of this is readily obtainable via the Internet

Other than that, the rest of the plan, its execution, and its resolution is all a complete work of fiction. It all came from a question I posed to myself after reading about ICANN and their fail-safe plan. It's one of those things you read and say "that is something out of a crazy spy novel or movie."

Well, you're right – and "viola" – an idea is born.

I'm sure there are those of you in the IT business that will read this work and say "bahh, that's all rubbish - that could never happen" or "he's got all of his facts wrong on how *xxxxx* works."

You're probably right. Remember, It's a work of **fiction** – just enjoy it and get over yourselves.

Acknowledgements

NaNoWriMo.org – for their brilliant idea and challenge of creating a short story/novel in 30 days. Without your forced deadlines, encouragement, and daily emails, I wouldn't have been able to complete this work. I tout your benefits to writers (and would-be writers) everywhere. You even got me to donate to your cause this year. Kudos to you.

Google – What can I say? It's the best search engine I've found. Need to see a map of Hong Kong? Google it. Need a Chinese translation? Google it. Need to find out where Burkina Faso is? Google it. I must have used Google hundreds of times during this project and it never let me down. It was especially helpful in the beginning, when I was looking up background on ICANN, their DNSSEC key-card plan, and other information (like worldwide internet routes). I was sure I was going to be placed on some government "watch list" for my searches, but so far, no one dressed in dark blue blazers and sunglasses has knocked on my door. Let's keep hoping.

My family – My wife, my mother, and my daughters have been nothing but encouraging throughout this entire process. November turns into a bit of a stressful month for Dad. The deadline looms and the word count must increase every day. Throughout it all, they have given me space to write, inquired about my daily word count, and been overall cheerleaders. It's almost Thanksgiving and I'm just finishing this up – well ahead of schedule. Thank you. My never ending love to you all.

Cover Design by www.ebooklaunch.com

About the Author

Besides writing novels and short stories, James R. Snyder works as a System Analyst for a major IT company. He lives in Western Maryland with his wife and two daughters.

www.ingramcontent.com/pod-product-compliance
Lightning Source LLC
Chambersburg PA
CBHW060538180626
46817CB00002B/631